Fallen Blades
Unwelcome Dreams

I0562347

Alex McHaddad

Copyright 2023 Alex McHaddad
All rights reserved
The characters and events portrayed in this
book are fictitious. Any similarity to real
persons, living or dead, is coincidental and not
intended by the author.
No part of this book may be reproduced, or
stored in a retrieval system, or transmitted in
any form or by any means, electronic,
mechanical, photocopying, recording, or
otherwise, without express written permission
of the publisher.

ISBN-13:
979-8-9856444-4-9

Library of Congress Control Number:
2023920840

Cover design by: Alex McHaddad
Printed in the United States of America

To Paulette.

Table of Contents

Prologue: Unwelcome History

It behooves the virtuous woman to understand the legacy she prolongs in raising a family in our fair Republic so that she may recite tales of the past to inspire the next generation to uphold our customs. Our history is full of strong women whose duty to their families enabled their husbands and sons to build the world we see today.

In eons past, the Skyborne descended from the heavens to tame the monsters and wilderness of our world. They brought with them the knowledge of the three great powers: Magic, Mechanics, and Nature, building a paradise that seemed destined to last forever. Yet the end inherited by all good things arrived much sooner than the Skyborne expected.

Long the enemy of the Skyborne, goblins ascended from the underworld and made war against our forebears, calling to their side the monsters once thought tamed. In their haste to retreat from this world, the Skyborne abandoned their children on the surface, under the care of those few young men and women who remained with their siblings. The elf maiden Janis Inglorien on the continent of Nova first built up a city as the children around her grew older, the first woman to raise a new generation into order and prosperity.

Among her greatest achievements, Janis counts the proper nurturing of her son Inglorn, who built the first ship of his generation and sailed the length of our world. Inglorn enlightened the generations of children who had grown up on every coast to the awakening promised by trade and diplomacy, leaving two Havens on every continent to guide new civilizations. As nations matured, the Havens of Inglorien renewed the practice of the Great Powers.

The Empire of Airgialla arose on an island off the coast of Nova, amassing power after fighting a devastating war against the kingdom of Burgundy. After conquering Burgundy, the Airgiallans used their newfound power and knowledge to wage war on every free nation rather than eliminate the goblins and monsters that lurked in the shadows. Inglorn's Havens were subdued, and their secrets emptied into the hands of Airgiallans, burgeoning their unbeatable arsenals. This lust for power consumed the Airgiallan men whose wives and mothers declined to educate their families in virtue, inviting corruption into every corner of the world.

This corruption manifested in the arrival of the Deathlords, demons who followed goblins out of the underworld and overcame the Airgiallans. Their noble women gave themselves over to the Deathlords, bearing children who could channel their power with a talisman. Absent virtue and possessed by darkness, the children of the Deathlords enacted draconian laws while encouraging depravity. These abominations reigned without contest for fifty years, growing ever more arrogant and drunk with fortune and authority.

Virtue remained firmly planted in the heart of Inglorn, who called upon his mother's teachings to stay strong in an Airgiallan prison. When the time was right, he escaped and led a crew of virtuous rebels in a campaign of destruction against the vessels that held together the Airgiallan empire. The deeds of his crew inspired others to join the Uprising, first among them the men of East Manifest, who ejected the Airgiallans west of the Frost Mountains and founded our dear Republic.

In Airgialla itself, the provincial queen Nikki rediscovered the merits of virtue and called upon the heavens for relief, receiving a sword forged by angels capable of striking down the talisman of the Deathlord children. After joining Inglorn's movement, Nikki struck down her corrupt kin and sank Airgialla beneath the waves. Her faithful followers retreated to the continent of Manifest and founded the New Airgiallan Empire.

The remaining children of the Deathlords fought hard against Nikki but could not withstand her assaults. Some retreated south, building mountains along the borders of the southern continents and draping the equatorial seas in the Enduring Storm. Empress Nikki bound the remaining children of the Deathlords in their strongholds, trapping them in the deserts of Cimmaron, the rainforests of southwest Manifest, the tundra of Nova, and the mountains of Shaolin. Last of all, Nikki drove the Locust, the greatest of the Deathlord children, into the dark continent of Legatus. She strapped the Locust's talisman to a boulder and dropped it into the middle of the ocean, never to be wielded by another soul.

These past nine hundred years since the Uprising have seen peace and prosperity blanket the Republic of East Manifest. While other nations *look to the restored Havens for guidance, we rely upon virtue to heal the wounds of the past and direct our affairs. As you lay your children down to sleep, you must warn them about the dangers of abandoning virtue but remind them that preservation is in their hands. Your sons shall wield swords when they must in its defense, but your daughters shall instill virtue into their families, and they must dream of no higher aim.*

~ A History of Virtue: From *Madame Wanda's Feminine Virtues*

Chapter 1: Unwelcome Lessons

A youth quivered in the chill mountain air as the headmaster slowly carved a switch. The more worried the youth grew, the colder the headmaster appeared as he droned on about philosophy.

"Virtue, children, has a cost. A brutal, unrelenting, ravenous cost. The screams of a rebel are meant to drive observers into the safe arms of conformity. And it is necessary because, outside the fold of society, one finds monsters who kill without cause. Violence is a part of both society and the wilderness, but in society, it is avoided by all who follow the rules. Nature shows no such compassion, killing indiscriminately even those who believe themselves in harmony."

Hope Defoe had stared longingly into that boy's eyes for weeks, smitten after he stopped to help her carry food home from the market. It was an innocent gesture, paired without further interaction, but Hope had pined for him ever since. Staring at him in class was just the first treat for her birthday.

"You're doing it again, birthday girl." Her friend Varsha had needled her that morning at the beginning of class. "He doesn't look any cuter today than yesterday."

"Yeah, but didn't you hear the joke he just told his friends?" Hope sighed happily and rested her face on her palm. "A sandwich walked into a tavern, and the barkeep said they don't serve food there! It's the first birthday gift anyone's given me today." She laughed out loud and stared in his direction, flipping her red hair in an attempt to grab his attention.

"Ugh, so pedestrian." Hope's friend Lauren didn't even look up from preparing her notes for the day.

Varsha stuck out her tongue. "Not all of us need to get our jokes from ancient plays. If it makes him laugh, leave him to it."

Lauren rolled her blue eyes. "I thought we'd want our best friend to fall for a man with a brain. Gareth is going to spend his days in the woods hauling timber. Want something better for yourself, Hope – Hope?"

"Hmm, what?" Hope broke her concentration. "Sorry, I can't stop thinking about him. Maybe if he likes me enough, he'll think about doing something more with his life. Apply to the National Academy, or become a constable."

Once again, Lauren's eyes retreated into her skull. "He'd be the only one from his class. You know how few people from this town make it to the National Academy, fewer still to the Haven Academy. We have to be perfect students just to apply."

As Lauren spoke, Varsha removed a stack of dollar bills from her pocket and absent-mindedly counted them. "Sorry, what was that? I was too busy thinking about getting into the National Academy."

Hope turned away from her friends and stared at her desk. "At least you'll be able to get out of this town. I'll be stuck with… whichever logger decides he wants a redhead in his home. For a second, I wanted to think someone wanted to be with me, not to be obligated to me."

Varsha was the first to put a hand on Hope's shoulder. "I know we don't have it easy as the only two women of foreign blood here. But remember, we're friends. You don't just throw away someone you've known since the cradle."

Lauren looked up from her books and nodded vigorously. "If Varsha and I go to Yorkton to study, you're coming! We couldn't imagine not seeing you every day. You'll have a place with us even if you're not attending the Academy."

The words failed to encourage Hope, and she stared again longingly at Gareth. "I'll work in a scullery while you go to school. It's not much of a life. At least here I'd only be washing dishes for one man and a few children…"

Before her friends could respond, their teacher came to the front of the class and wrapped a stick on the chalkboard. "Good morning, class."

"Good morning, Miss Jolene."

"A moment of silence for your personal devotions."

Every head in the class bowed, some praying and some taking an extra moment to sleep. For most, it was a show of conformity... perhaps why Gareth wasn't joining in. Hope surreptitiously squinted behind her folded hands, curiosity piqued by his decision to rock his head side to side.

Miss Jolene was disturbed. "Class, you must all be respectful. Perhaps we need another moment."

Unperturbed, Gareth began tapping on his desk, drawing a glare from the teacher that he deftly ignored.

The crack of the pointer on the chalkboard shocked everyone to attention. "Alright, class, time to pledge allegiance to the Republic." Everyone in the room except for Gareth stood up and faced the flag of the Republic of Manifest, reciting the banal oath of fealty to their homeland.

Pursing her lips, Miss Jolene looked for a way to maintain classroom decorum. "Would anyone like to remind us why we pledge our allegiance daily? Hope?"

The stares of the entire class pierced Hope like daggers. "Um... to remind ourselves of our duties as citizens?"

Miss Jolene nodded. "Yes, citizens. Remember, this Republic is home to all who wish to be here, and we must be grateful for that. Hope Defoe's parents are obviously from New Airgialla, the Imperium that once enslaved our lands. She would be a queen just over the border, looking down on those around her. In our country, she merely sees fellow citizens. Or take the Bharat – Varsha could only remain there because her hair and skin are dark, but in the Republic –"

Varsha noisily made a show of pulling out her stack of bills and flipping through them before suddenly looking up at Miss Jolene. "Sorry, I couldn't hear you over the sound of my mother's contribution to the school's summer re-thatching."

Miss Jolene cringed for a moment before turning her ire toward Gareth. "You know the Republic's Constitution protects free expression, Gareth, but you're setting a bad example for the class. How virtuous do you think your protest truly is, young man?"

Gareth simply laughed. "Independence is my favorite virtue, Miss Jolene. After all, the Mayor has decided my family should be independent of food by taxing homes without a male head of household. My father abandoned us, and we're paying the price."

Miss Jolene scoffed. "A virtuous woman would have found a new husband. There is no shortage of assistance to rebuild a family so broken, and she knows that. More money is needed to take care of families without a father. The Society of Virtue has gladly offered to help your mother find a suitor, but she always denies the help. You ought to be allegiant to your Republic for its allegiance to you, even if your mother rejects our society. Now go see the headmaster and explain yourself."

Gareth burst into laughter. "The headmaster can come get me; I'm here to learn. You're not nearly this passionate when teaching us about reading and arithmetic."

Miss Jolene huffed and turned toward one of Gareth's friends. "Clyde, go fetch the headmaster and tell him everything." Clyde tried to object, but he feared the fire in Miss Jolene's eyes. Grimacing, Clyde left the room as the class sat in an increasingly awkward silence.

The next few moments were numbing. The headmaster arrived shortly with Clyde and a pair of constables in tow. When Gareth refused to follow the headmaster to his office, he was violently pulled from his seat as the headmaster's ravings assaulted the class's ears.

Miss Jolene ordered the class to follow, her spectacles fogging as she grew unnerved by the ferocity she knew she would witness. A pit filled Hope's stomach as she prepared to watch the object of her affection take lashes for his insolence. Varsha at first stayed behind, shielded by her mother's coin, but changed her mind when her friends turned to look at her with eyes full of despair.

Hope tried to stand at the back of the crowd of students, but Miss Jolene grabbed her arm and forced her to stand at the front with Gareth's friends. The teacher knew far more about her students than she cared to reveal, and she was putting her observations to painful use.

The headmaster seemed to draw to a close as the switch was carved painfully thin. "What little order is found in nature comes from the same force that holds together a family. As the wise man said, it's a father's duty to train up a child in the way that he should go. Yours abandoned you, and that's no fault of your own. Had he stayed, you would have learned that a father wields the rod so that others are not forced to. Disciplining you is a solemn honor, one that you will come to thank me for."

Gareth groaned as the constables slammed his shirtless body onto a damp tree stump, followed by piercing shrieks as the headmaster emotionlessly struck his back. Hope couldn't squeeze her friends' hands, but when she tried to turn to Lauren and Varsha for some looks of reassurance, Miss Jolene forcefully turned her head toward Gareth. The message was for men and women – conform to the greater power around you. Men were to bend to the will of their society, and women were to bend to the will of their men. A chill greater than the late winter air could muster shook Hope's spine as she thought about what her children would endure if this didn't change. But what could one person do?

"They can stop now." Hope weakly whispered into Miss Jolene's ear.

"Say that again for the whole class!" The headmaster paused as everyone turned toward a speechless Hope. "You didn't just order your headmaster to refrain from disciplining a student, did you?"

Hope cringed at a groaning Gareth before looking at the ground, fearing the pain that would follow if she stood up for her classmate. "It isn't virtuous to speak out of turn. I should have waited to be addressed, just like *Madame Wanda's Feminine Virtues* prescribes."

The headmaster broke his switch in two and dropped the pieces. "Well done, Miss Jolene. I see the rot in this boy's head has not spread to your other students. They may return to your tutelage."

Hope stood still as the students were led back into class, dragged away only by the force of Lauren and Varsha. She watched in horror as a constable ripped Gareth's shirt in half, and the headmaster shook his head when he tried to walk back inside.

Lauren tried to comfort Hope as they filtered into the halls on the way to their classroom. "Just one more year of school, and we won't have to deal with this again."

Varsha offered a weak smile. "It's sixteenth birthday, you can drown your sorrows in cake tonight. It's supposed to be a secret, but your grandfather booked a feast for you at the tavern."

The specter of celebration offered Hope little joy. "The only thing I want for my birthday is the courage to speak up, to say what's right. Every part of what happened just now was wrong. I was just the only one foolish enough to think I could stop it."

Lauren patted her on the back. "Well, you have a wish to make tonight. Dream of a world where the right thing is never unwelcome and know that your friends share that dream."

Manny nervously scanned the pews across the Greystone Haven Cathedral, worried that one of the parishioners would recognize him. Mid-day during the week was a time when only the most pious gathered to pray and meditate, and there was a chance that they knew even the faces of the congregants who attended worship just one day per week. It would typically benefit the son of the County Sheriff to be seen as devout – but in his uncertain times, sharing company with a wizard could bring unfavorable attention.

"You make eye contact with anyone else here, you just might cause a scandal!" The laughter of the Vicar caught Manny off guard.

Manny chuckled nervously in reply. "I hoped the hood over my eyes would do some good. My father, of all people, taught me well how to avoid being seen, Father Jerome."

The Vicar's countenance stiffened suddenly. "Manny, I'll have to ask you again. You're sure your father is comfortable with this meeting? I'm surprised he'd risk giving the Judge an attack of nerves over this."

"Yes." Manny smiled as best he could, barely winning an argument in his head once more. "He's always said that every young man needs to find his own path. We're glad the Haven Cathedral will help us navigate the waters ahead." It was true enough for the moment. Most of the young men Manny's age were attending a spiritual retreat in preparation for their rite of manhood, due to begin an apprenticeship or attend an academy after the coming summer. Unlike the rest, Manny had a unique vocation that needed to be tested.

"I'm no magician, son." Father Jerome put a hand on Manny's shoulder as he joined him on the pew. "But I know miracles only come easy when your heart is at peace. I've watched you grow into a fine young man only because of your father's care. If you've hidden this from him, you may not wind up on your desired path."

The Vicar's words evinced a frown on Manny's face. "How many people can simply sit down to dinner with their parents and claim they can perform magic? It's not impossible, but it's so rare that it'll simply fetch a laugh! Besides, my father has always expected me to join him in the constabulary. If I tell him I want to be an Enchanter, he'll need proof that I have the gift. Only a wizard can do that, Father."

Father Jerome trumpeted a long sigh. "The power within every Enchanter comes from above, son. A wizard will see what I have seen. But your father is a better man than you give him credit for, and that's not a good enough reason to hide your gift. Perhaps writing to the Haven was a bad idea after all…"

Manny's eyes popped. "Father, you can't go back now! The wizard is nearly here, he will be annoyed that you summoned him for nothing!"

Father Jerome shrugged. "That's for me to worry about, son, and I'll make peace with his anger. But an Enchanter will be far angrier to find out that his ward isn't authorized to be trained than he is that a prospect skipped a meeting."

Unable to help slumping back in his pew, Manny rubbed his eyes. "My father will never let me leave for a Haven to study magic. If I stay here, my destiny is to wield a spear, not a staff, and my gift will be for nothing."

Father Jerome shook his head fiercely. "You need to stop thinking in worldly terms, son. You know the right thing to do is to tell your father. The power flowing through your veins stems from the same authority that defines honesty and integrity. This gift will only be wasted if you do not choose to do what is right."

"Pardon me, Father Jerome?" The interruption came from a bald man with a gray beard and garish clothes.

"May I help you, friend?" Father Jerome stood up and extended a hand in greeting.

The man bowed his head. "Yes, I'm Christopher Deas from Byeong's Haven. I've been sent to evaluate a young Enchanter."

Father Jerome's hand went limp, and he pulled away. "Excuse me, did you say Byeong's Haven? You'll forgive my surprise, but why send an Enchanter from the other side of the world when Angela's Haven is but a few days' ride from here?"

Christopher nodded in understanding. "Some of that is Haven business. But you understand the dispute your Republic is having with the Havens – one of Angela's Enchanters would have difficulty getting around the country. I had business here anyway and was asked to make the journey. Besides, I was told that sending someone my status would be well received."

"You don't know how much!" Manny sensed an opportunity to curry favor, standing up to awkwardly shake the Enchanter's hand. "Governor Deas, Manny Alonso. My father is the Sheriff of Greystone and a close confidant of Judge Craven. We're the only province left in favor of diplomacy with the Havens, and your presence will be seen as a true honor."

Christopher blushed. "Perhaps you can arrange dinner with the Judge on my return. Lady Angela will be pleased to know she still has an ally."

Manny raised an eyebrow. "Your... return, sir?"

Christopher nodded. "Yes, this was to be but a brief stop along my way to the home of an old friend. I can send a recommendation for further review if you prove your power. We'll need the permission of your parents to study enchantments, as I'm sure the Vicar has explained."

Father Jerome pursed his lips. "I've explained in great detail. Manny can tell you all about it, I'm sure."

The assertion made Manny gulp. "Oh, um, yes, I, um, he, has..."

"Is something the matter, boy?" Christopher raised an eyebrow.

"Well, Governor..." Manny paused for a moment to consider his words carefully. What he did in this moment would determine the course of his whole life. "Governor, I haven't spoken with my father yet. Yes, Greystone's court favors the Havens, but magic has faded so much from daily life that just suggesting that study of enchantments to my father will be met with ridicule. I wanted someone else to evaluate me and verify my fitness so that he knows I'm serious."

Christopher tapped his beard briefly, studying Manny's worried eyes and Jerome's annoyed smirk. "Father Jerome, I assume you think Manny is going about this all the wrong way. Truthfully, the Vicar of my old parish looked at me just the same when I revealed my gift. I know what it's like to have a pragmatic father disapprove of magic, worried about the distraction from the real world. This young man couldn't be in better company."

Farmer Jerome relaxed, but his expression remained staid. "I'll let you two speak. Manny, it's on you to be truthful with your father. Don't expect my approval or assistance." The Vicar's words stung, and Manny had trouble remaining upbeat as the Enchanter took Father Jerome's place on the pew.

Christopher seemed to readily recognize Manny's troubles. "The Vicar shows good judgment, my boy. But you need not share his fear. I wrestled for years with the decision to become an Enchanter without my father's blessing, and I won't let you share my struggle. If you truly possess the gift of miracles, there is no better place for you than Angela's Haven."

The Enchanter's encouragement allowed Manny to finally relax. "Thank you, Governor. He gave me quite the moral quandary. Now, how do you verify my gift?"

The Enchanter smirked. "Very easy, cast a spell on demand and let the magic do its work for you!"

There was no stopping the muscles in Manny's neck from tightening. "Um, you see, I can't quite do it like that, sir. It's not something that happens on demand; it's reactive. Sometimes, I get an impulse to act. Other times, I see a situation where magic can help, and I ask for the power to flow through me."

A gargantuan smile perched on Christopher's face. "Nobody I've trained has ever captured the spirit of enchanting so quickly! Too many believe that there's a simple trick to it that they don't quite know. Perhaps the strength of their convictions, the memorization of a particular spell, or a relationship with the divine that gets them whatever they want just for the asking. True enchantments come from above, not from within ourselves."

This news brightened Manny's smile for a moment, but a shifting of his lips soon invited worry. "Well, it's good to know that I'm not broken. I thought perhaps I was just new and needed training to summon a miracle. But it begs the question of how you can determine whether I have the gift at all."

Christopher nodded. "It's different for every person. The word of a Vicar is enough to invite evaluation but not enough to secure tutelage. In Father Jerome's letter, he speaks of fire. But you don't seem fiery or destructive. And that's another reason I believe you have a gift – I'm guessing that when you conjure flame, the power terrifies you, leaves you cautious about its use?"

A passing lady caught Manny's attention, frills and feathers from her hat drawing uncomfortably near candles lining the wall. Eyes widening, Manny obeyed a drive to whisk an adjacent flame away just as it would have lit a piece of fabric. The woman was none the wiser, but Christopher appeared impressed.

"I've seen enough." The Enchanter stood up from the pew and offered Manny a hand. "You'll learn to seek discernment as you draw closer to the divine. It was not that woman's destiny today to burn, just as it was not mine to walk out of this Cathedral without a new Enchanter."

Jumping to his feet, Manny shook Christopher's hand vigorously. "You have no idea how much I wanted to hear that, Governor! If we can visit my father now, I'm sure he will hear your words and allow me to move to Angela's Haven."

The Enchanter raised an eyebrow. "Does he expect you home during the Rite of Manhood?"

"No, but I'm sure it will be –"

"Let's take some extra time, you and I." Christopher appeared excited. "I mentioned I'm traveling on Haven business. Perhaps you'd like to join?"

Such a development had not been among Manny's hopes, and he seized the opportunity. "When do we leave? I can pack my bags at once!"

"I'll be taking my lunch at the Hirose Hotel. Meet me once you've packed your bags. And bring a sword just in case; with the number of goblin attacks on the road, we can't afford to be too careful." The Enchanter shook Manny's hand, and they parted ways.

Manny ran to his house, unoccupied by his ever-busy father, and packed light for a journey on the road. The armory presented the only problem – he could choose from a sword he had purchased himself or a cutlass gifted by his father. Once again, Manny found himself choosing between his own path or his father's. After a moment, he reached for the cutlass and promised himself that he would be honest with his father. The journey with the Enchanter would merely delay the conversation, and Manny was not simply another runaway. His father would always be part of him, no matter the path he followed, and the road would allow him to prepare for the next phase of their relationship.

"This one yours?" A drunk merchant's rank breath filled the air of a smoky tavern.

"Leave us." Hikaru had no wish to fight the man who mistook his assistant, Yukio, for a prostitute.

"Never been with an elf before, I'll pay top dollar." He shook a pair of coins in his hand.

"Leave us, this is your final warning." Hikaru frowned and placed his hand on the hilt of his sword.

The trader growled. "Shoulda never expected so much from a foreigner, y'all hate us anyway!"

Taking a swig of beer from his mug, the trader spat it toward Hikaru's assistant, only for his eyes to widen at the sight of the liquid gathering into a ball in the air. Hikaru smirked as he drew the rest of the beer into the air, the dinner crowd turning toward the display after the merchant's mug clattered on the floor. As the merchant tried to back away, he fretted at his beer snaking around him.

"Strike me, you can keep your whore! Meant nothing by it, elf!" The merchant nervously placed his hand on a knife hilt.

Hikaru was livid. "You dare to call a civil servant of the Naran diplomatic corps a whore?" He jumped from his seat and reformed the beer into an oval clamped onto the man's face, sealing his nostrils and mouth.

"Alright, that's enough!" The barkeep stomped toward the pair as the merchant fell to the ground, spitting out the beer left in his mouth after Hikaru released the spell.

Hikaru glared at the barkeep. "You should know better than to allow your customers to be so molested. Assaulting a diplomat is a grievous crime."

"Molested? Ma'am, this fellow didn't even touch you!" The barkeep put his hands on his hips. "Can't kick you out now, but you best be out before the next Sheriff's patrol arrives from Greystone. Ain't nobody fancy enough to keep from going to prison for using magic like that. Might just add more to your tab to clean up the mess!"

Hikaru raised an eyebrow. "What mess?" He hid his satisfaction as the barkeep looked down to see the floor and the merchant's clothes miraculously dry.

The barkeep frowned. "Ugh, I'm keeping my eye on you. You pay for this fellow's room, and we'll be even."

Hikaru shook his head. "On the contrary, our lodging will be free. My family has owned taverns for fifteen hundred years, and you will not live to see 75. When a guest is assaulted, you accommodate them, or you lose business."

Yukio stood up and nodded. "Minister Hirose will make a formal complaint to the Sheriff if I ask him. You don't want to scare away customers, do you?"

Feigning fear for a moment, the barkeep threw back his head and left. "It's a five-day ride across these mountains, one hotel per day. Nobody has a choice. I'll let you both off easy; keep your distance from this fellow, and no more magic."

Shrugging, Hikaru sat back in his chair by the fireplace as Yukio joined him. "This Republic was not so vile in younger days. It has been corrupted by lies, propaganda that this nation is self-sufficient. Every man is told that he has the power to take what he wants from those around him. Yukio, this corruption comes from somewhere and must be rooted out before it's too late."

Yukio scratched her head. "Perhaps because the Haven churches have been pushed out. You remember how the President cursed them when we met with him and Ambassador Suzuki. The teachings in his "free churches" are far different than what the Haven churches preach."

Hikaru pursed his lips. "An absence of what is good can allow evil to rise, yes, but there is something else. I sensed it in the air when we crossed the border. Something is wrong with this nation, something that Angela's Haven could fix if the Republic had not grown so hostile."

Yukio leaned forward to whisper. "Do you think, perhaps, a witch or warlock has begun corrupting the land? It would explain the increase in goblin attacks in the hill country that Ambassador Suzuki described."

It was an astute hypothesis, tempting Hikaru to smile despite the gravity of the situation. "I would not doubt it. Goblins have little agency on their own. It takes a storm of dark magic to command them, which is why their armies never stray far from Deathlord strongholds. In the wilderness, they are untamed, roving, chaotic. If Ambassador Suzuki is correct, something is controlling the goblins, and the Republic is doing what it can to prepare its people for war. They have forgotten that their laws are what inspired their people to fight for freedom, not a heritage or a culture, and they will find it is only their first love that will win the day."

Hiding a smile in gratitude at her mentor's validation, Yukio bowed her head in appreciation before continuing. "Tell me, Minister, you used to be an Enchanter. Angela's Haven must investigate despite the Republic's hostility. Why have we seen no Enchanters outside the Haven Academy in Yorkton?"

Hikaru sighed. "Perhaps because their greatest Enchanter left them ten years ago."

This startled Yukio. "You mean Governor Christopher of Byeong's Haven? Your old friend?"

Hikaru nodded. "Few see his gift of discernment surpassed. If anyone could uncover the mystery, it would be him. But, this must be left to the Haven. Our duty is to report the conditions of the Republic to the Empress so that our merchants may travel here safely. It is not our job to make the Republic safe for them or anyone else. If these people prefer isolation, that shall be their fate.

"Hey, read the sign! No new visitors past nightfall! There's goblins in these woods!" The barkeep's shout at the barred door shook the room as though he believed a goblin was on the other side of the entrance.

The response on the other side was muffled, but Hikaru felt he understood the voice clearly. Closing his eyes, he felt for the vapor in the air by the door and lifted the bar from its place as the barkeep nervously huffed about dark magic. The door slid open as an Enchanter entered with a young servant in tow.

"It's a warlock! Get out of here!" The barkeep raised a butcher knife as visitors crowded around the door. Hikaru closed his eyes again and found his ears assaulted by the sound of horrid coughing from the group a moment later. Approaching the barkeep, he stood in front of the visitor.

"Sir, this is no warlock seeking to let goblins into your inn. This is my old friend Christopher Deas of Byeong's Haven, and you will treat him with the honor he deserves." Hikaru smirked at the barkeep, who nodded through his cough and struggled to bar the door again.

"Hirose Hikaru, it has been far too long!" Christopher bowed his head in reverence. "I never thought I'd see you in this old place. I assume you're representing Her Majesty?"

"Wait, not old Enchanter Christopher?" The barkeep interrupted and vigorously shook the Enchanter's hand. "It's me, Danny! Remember? I bought this place from old Jameson a few years ago when he retired!"

Christopher smiled warmly. "I'll never forget your cocktails – nothing else worth tipping for in the hill country. Can you still mix a Karelia mule?"

"Four coming up on the house!" The barkeep disappeared behind the bar.

Hikaru raised his eyebrow. "Ah, the Republic. I forgot that coin is the coin of this land." He and Christopher shared a laugh while the Enchanter's acolyte looked puzzled. "Come join me by the fire."

As they sat down, introductions were exchanged. Christopher's acolyte, a potential apprentice, did his best to hide his awe in the presence of two storied Enchanters. He showed enough potential for Christopher's attention, but Hikaru quickly observed that Manny was not without his faults. The more they sipped on their cocktails, the more auspicious glances Manny cast at Yukio.

"So, Manny Alonso… related to Greystone Sheriff Juan Alonso?" Hikaru sipped his drink as Manny confirmed his parentage. "He's new to Greystone, I understand. 15 years since both of you arrived from Castille – oh, don't be surprised, young man. As the Chief Minister in Manifest for Nara, it is my business to know everyone."

"And…what is your business, Yukio?" Manny could barely hide what should have been a forbidden fascination.

Hikaru was quick to answer. "She is my assistant, taking notes about my travels. Yukio will help write a report on Manifest that will be read throughout Nara."

Yukio smiled. "Thanks to the Minister, I will gain renown that will allow me to join a more hallowed house. Few people born as commoners have a chance to join the nobility."

"Ah. That's – that's wonderful! We don't have nobility in Manifest; here, we rise because of our ability." Manny likely knew he would never achieve Yukio's romantic favor and transitioned back to reality rather quickly.

"Besides my notes of this trip, she is working on a special manuscript. My memoirs of the War of Four Emperors." Hikaru expected Manny to be impressed, but he was shocked by a look of horror on the young man's face. "Are you ill, young man?"

"Well…" Manny stared awkwardly at Christopher, who appeared equally uneasy. "The Republic and Doryian are allies, so you can imagine that we don't… favorably learn about the war in school. One of the first stories we read as children is *We Thought We Would Be Heroes*. But… well, I don't know your role in that war, Minister. I'm sure you were one of the good ones."

Hikaru could not help scowling. "Good ones? What good ones? We led armies of half-breeds to war against goblins because they are also beasts, feral and vicious toward all around them. The races don't mix, young man. The product of an unholy union can never be made holy, and that war is proof. The half-breeds call their little land of Doryian a nation, but it is merely a buffer against goblins, savagery matched by savagery."

Yukio appeared crestfallen, and a subtle nod from Hikaru gave her license to speak. "The things the Minister saw would make anyone sick. The half-breeds, they are full of darkness. One cannot come from two worlds and be one; it tears their hearts apart in the womb. Those who do not see suspect nothing. The Minister's memoirs will open eyes to the truth."

Hikaru nodded in approval. "How many half-breeds do you know, young man?"

The question startled Manny. "Well, none, really-"

"Exactly." Hikaru smirked. "The alliance with Manifest is one of convenience. Your leaders do not like the half-breeds half as much as they claim. Any spawn of an unholy union is sent straight to Doryian. Most countries deport them anyway, but the leaders of your Republic like to coat it with an air of dignity."

"That can't… that can't be right…" Manny's dissonance begged a laughter that Hikaru knew would be unbecoming.

Christopher attempted to awkwardly steer the conversation away. "You see, Manny, not everything is quite so clear cut. The War of Four Emperors and its aftermath are both far more complicated than can be distilled for a schoolbook. Values change throughout history, and people must only do the best they can with the information they have at the time. The alliance between Manifest and Doryian is far more politically expedient for the Republic than it is for the half-breeds. Doryian accepts it because they have few other friends. That's why people must write what they know, so that the whole of the story can be considered before an opinion is made."

Manny raised an eyebrow. "And what is your opinion?"

Christopher mumbled to himself for a moment. "Oh, strike me, I didn't wander here to debate the War of the Four Emperors. But.. It is providential that we met Hikaru in these hills. If you're here, old friend, I assume you've already met with President Pilcher and know about the goblin attacks."

Hikaru nodded, shielding disappointment that Christopher did not delve further into his complicated opinions on the war. "Something, someone or some force, is coordinating them. This far from the nearest Deathlord stronghold makes that news truly terrifying for Naran merchants. Trade with the Republic will decrease substantially if Angela's Haven cannot contain it. I assume that's why they sent you."

Christopher laughed. "Only the best!"

"Of course! But what can you find at such an ersatz establishment?"

Christopher winked. "You remember my old friend Caleb Defoe?"

"Of course! The greatest historian of his generation. Does he yet live? He departed Angela's Haven years ago in obscurity rather than celebration."

Christopher took a deep breath. "Yes, and when he left, he took a manuscript on talismans that was never published. My copy was destroyed by a careless longshoreman at Byeong's Haven. I'll wager there is no more complete a compendium on the subject anywhere else in the Hemisphere. He lives in a village a day's ride west of here, town called Braddock. If anyone can help me uncover the mystery, it's him. Hopefully, we can find whatever witch got her hand on a talisman and bring it to Angela's Haven for study."

Hikaru sat back momentarily, crossing his arms as he carefully considered Christopher's words. "You know, I told Yukio earlier that fixing this problem is not our job. But I am not so arrogant to think that the situation could never have required my intervention. I cannot bring my retinue that far off the highway, nor can I leave them, Christopher, but I can help you once you bring me a copy of the manuscript. It would be in the interest of Nara for the Republic to be defended from resurgent goblins. We would not want their filth to spread if it is what you suspect."

Christopher turned toward Manny and smiled. "Few Enchanters embark on a quest so important as this their first time in the field, Manny. Even fewer are blessed for the tutelage of a statesman like Hikaru."

Hikaru smiled. "You are too kind, my young friend. It is I who shall be honored to join you. The man to whom the world owes a debt must not expect to be repaid." He caught a look of admiration from Manny, knowing that a hundred such looks from the right people would finally get him the honor he deserved.

Chapter 2: Unwelcome Wizard

"So, what exactly is a talisman?" After listening to Christopher pontificate for days, Manny reasoned that he had earned the right to ask at least one question.

Christopher's head reared in surprise. "Well, I thought you would have deduced it by now! It's the weapon of one of the Deathlords, imbued with their power and only meant to be used by their descendants, the Fallen."

Manny nodded. "Does it have to be by a direct descendant, or can any one of them use another's talisman? Are the powers all the same, or are they different?"

Christopher shrugged. "That's where my familiarity ends. Thus, the journey to such a secluded village. Braddock, Manifest. Who would have thought such a little town could play such a pivotal role in world history."

Manny surveyed the small town around them, desperately avoiding eye contact with the villagers gawking at the garishly dressed Enchanter. "Pivotal? Aren't we just going to borrow a book?"

Christopher threw back his head and laughed. "My boy, we're on the cusp of an adventure! Live as long as I have, you can smell it in the air! You're hoping to come into your own as a man when along comes a mentor to show you the way. A journey to a small town to collect intelligence on an enemy, that's merely the first step. We'll be on our way to rooting out the evil in the hill country soon enough. You can prove to your father that you're ready to leave home and become an Enchanter, and I'll return to Byeong's Haven with a tale to inspire the other initiates who cross my path."

The Enchanter's prediction made Manny's heart skip a beat. "You make it sound so easy, sir wizard -"

"Don't you dare call me that!" Christopher suddenly grew uncharacteristically livid.

Manny cringed. "Pardon me, isn't that just another word for Enchanter?"

Sighing, Christopher mustered a small. "When the Deathlords controlled our world, their enforcers were known as wizard. Those who remember save that word as an insult, casting the stone at those who seek to use magic for their own ends."

Nothing noteworthy escaped Manny's sight as he squinted. "Apologies, Christopher. But I can't help but ask, how does an Enchanter summon magic for his own ends? All power flows from the divine; how can it be corrupted by selfish motives?"

The question transformed Christopher's frustration into melancholy. "I have seen it too many times. Not all adventures end in victory. Sometimes, people fall to their own greed, lust, avarice... It is the will of the divine that their sins be used for good, even when their hearts are in the wrong place. I'd want for you to never come across it, but you must be prepared to see it. The Haven will show you the way."

For a moment, the stormy sky grew even darker as Manny began to doubt the Enchanter's strength of character for the first time. Christopher had seemed grand, lofty, and composed, yet he allowed himself to fall apart in front of someone he barely knew. There was a line of familiarity one needed to approach before sharing such an intimate sense of disappointment, and the Enchanter had gone nowhere near it.

"Ah, here we are!" Christopher halted his horse in front of a well-kept but small shack near the edge of town. "Even at Angela's Haven, you'd be lucky to meet someone as renowned as my dear old friend. Not sure if he's home, but no matter. He always let me in."

A tinge of nervousness struck Manny as he looked down the lane and saw a few anxious townsfolk heading in his direction, likely the prelude to a visit from the constable. He could simply show his father's seal and escape danger, but avoiding conflict where the Haven was involved was better. The national government would use any excuse to subsume Greystone's autonomy, and nepotism could finally instigate that desired subjugation.

Creaking door hinges assaulted Manny's ears as he and the Enchanter crossed the threshold. "Surprised your friend didn't lock the door if this book is so valuable."

Christopher chuckled. "Perhaps he thinks the distance from civilization is security enough. Small towns like this, the people stick together far more than in the cities. Nobody fights for them if they don't fight for each other."

It seemed as good an explanation as any. "I'll check the shelf on the left for the manuscript if you'll check on the right." Manny marched toward a nearby bookcase without awaiting the Enchanter's reply. He was shocked by the quality and age of the manuscripts before him, most notably a copy of the famed biography *Jasmine the Wanderer*. What surprised him more was the realization that most of the volumes were fiction, and he began to wonder if they were indeed in the home of a historian.

The Enchanter seemed to have more luck. "Ah, here it is! *A Treatise on Talismans*, by Caleb Defoe."

"And meant for his private library!" The raging yell that shook the house impossibly emanated from a short man with snowy white hair.

Christopher winked at Manny, then cringed at the man before smiling widely. "It has been far too long, old friend."

The smile that Christopher hoped to see on the old man never arrived. "What in the name of the world are you doing here? It's been ten years since you wrote to us! Did you really think you could march back into my home and steal my books? Oh, it's a wonder I ever trusted you! Boy," he finished glaring at Manny, "best find a new master, this one will never keep his word."

Blinking, Manny grew worried by the despair on Christopher's face. "Mr. Defoe, I don't know what this Enchanter did to you, but he's trying to make the world a better place. We only came to find a manuscript that-"

"Ha!" The old man shook his head. "He had a far greater chance than anyone in a thousand years. Threw it all away once he got his big promotion. He's made it clear that he doesn't need me."

"No, you need me!" Christopher slammed the butt of his staff onto the floor. "*They* need me, old friend. Angela's Haven has discerned that the goblins attacking the hill country bend toward the will of one master. You don't want *them* in harm's way. I know what I have done wrong. I can never absolve myself, but you must allow me but one act of penance. Help me rid the hill country of these monsters, and I shall go in peace."

Tears began to fall from the old man's eyes. "You're too late for that. Daniel died last fall when they came for us. We weren't prepared... *they* weren't prepared."

Awkward eyes disrupted the argument as Manny raised his hand. "Pardon me, Mr. Defoe, who are you talking about, exactly?"

Caleb huffed. "Not much of a concern of yours, boy. You'll be back on the road shortly. Don't worry about my family."

"The choice isn't yours." Christopher's words caught Caleb off guard. "Flora and Terry have as much to say as you. Terry especially, who might still be going home to a husband if I had trained them properly. You know I owe Daniel that much."

Caleb rolled his eyes. "Don't tell me the Governor of Magic at a Haven wasn't surrounded by women! Was that why you stayed away? You were pining away for a married woman, and you just couldn't stand to see her with Daniel?"

Christopher shrank back meekly. "I will admit that was part of it. More so, my duties at the Haven. An annual trip to Manifest would invite questions and draw followers. Eventually, they would be discovered. Even letters could be intercepted to their detriment. There was no other way."

A careful silence allowed Caleb to collect his thoughts. "After a while, we agreed it was for the best. You abandoning your promise. For the first time in generations, they are at peace. Sure, a small mountain town is no grand city, and their lives are far from luxurious. But they are comfortable, and that is enough. They'll marry, have children here, and then pass on like their forebears. Age or the plague shall do them in rather than the sword. They think they'll go to Yorkton when they're older to study at a university, but we've always planned to hold them here. The goblins are just the perfect excuse, so we truly have no quarrel with them. Daniel's killers were hunted down, so that matter is closed. The days are getting darker, wizard. We'll shield them as long as possible and let destiny give their children the choice of living in peace or living up to their... heritage..."

Manny leaped to Caleb's side and helped him onto a couch as he began to gasp for air. "Are you ill, sir? Christopher, help him!"

"Thank you, my boy. I'm not ill, just old." Caleb sighed. "Now Christopher, you see my point, don't you? I can't argue much more. Just leave now before I have to fetch a constable. I won't even tell Terry and Flora about your bad judgment."

Christopher took the unexpected step of kneeling before his friend. "We always knew the days would get darker, but we were not left powerless against it. God gave us three young women whose blood carried the courage of a lion, the wisdom of an owl, the shrewdness of a wolf-"

"I hate this town!" The shout came from a blur of red hair atop a green dress that slammed open the front door and vanished into the hallway.

Caleb sighed deeply. "I challenge you to find a young lady with the shrewdness of a shrew, let alone a wolf. Have you ever seen anyone so upset on their own birthday?"

This took Christopher aback. "Is it really Hope's birthday? My, how she has grown!"

"Shall we fetch her?" Manny tried to hide his fascination with the young lady who had stormed by. "If you get dizzy spells like this, I mean, she'll know best how to help you, right?"

Caleb sat back in thought for a moment. "Perhaps it'll be good for you to meet them after all."

A smile curved around Christopher's lips. "Nothing would delight me more, old friend. I know I should have been here for them, and they probably have no memory of me. If you'll help me with the matter of the talisman, I may even be able to see to it that they are trained properly at Angela's Haven. It's what Gina would have wanted for her daughter, after all."

"What was that about my mother?" The young lady suddenly appeared from the hallway carrying a tray of cookies with mugs and a jar of milk.

Caleb glared and surreptitiously shook his head at Christopher. "Nothing, dear. I'm sure you misheard this fellow."

Hope set down her tray on a coffee table and began pouring milk. "Please, grandfather, I've had a rough day. A story about my mother might be just what I need. You don't really want me to be sad for my birthday dinner, do you?"

Caleb fell back into his chair, suffocating a rising scowl. "Of course not! Why do you think I invited a wizard? He's full of tricks, master of the unexpected. Does quite the disappearing act."

Christopher got up from the floor and walked towards the young lady, shaking her hand before grabbing a cookie and a mug. "You are Hope, I take it?"

Hope did her best to speak through a mouthful of dessert. "Pleased to meet you, sir wizard!"

"Oh please, call me Christopher!" The Enchanter turned and snuck a glare at Caleb before taking his seat on another couch. "Manny, aren't you hungry?"

The Enchanter's question shook Manny out of the trance that had overtaken him since he laid eyes on Hope. "Uh, why, yes." He took a mug and a cookie, sitting beside Christopher before eagerly biting into the cookie. It was hard and a little stale, but he mustered a smile. "These are excellent, thank you!" Hope smiled weakly.

Caleb finally grabbed his own treat and settled back onto the couch. "Hope, this is Christopher Deas and his… apprentice, I guess? Actually, you never introduced us."

Manny stood up and bowed. "Manuel Alonso of Greystone. Pleased to meet all of you." Wanting to get Hope's attention, he added, "M-my father is the, uh, Sheriff of Greystone."

Caleb's eyes widened. "So that's why you're being tutored by a Haven Governor! You're not nearly assertive enough to get such a master on your own."

Manny frowned. "That has nothing to do with it! I've never used my father's position to get what I want. He doesn't even know I'm training with an Enchanter!"

Caleb was unimpressed. "Hiding from your parents is the start of a lot of pain. I'm surprised Christopher hasn't imparted that lesson yet."

Christopher huffed. "Far more important things are afoot. You know full well why we're here."

Hope sighed. "Guessing you're not really here for my birthday, then?"

Caleb winked. "Actually, it's the wizard here who's come for a lesson, let's say in humility. I met him many years ago, Terry and Flora, too. But you can rest assured, he'll provide some fabulous entertainment."

Hope raised an eyebrow. "I suppose I don't have any say in it. Just glad my friends will be there."

Manny raised his hand to interject but simply drew Caleb's laughter. "Why in the name of the world are you raising your hand, boy? You're not in school!"

Hope smiled. "Well, I think it's sweet. Such manners are… virtuous."

Caleb frowned. "On second thought, perhaps you ought to leave. As much as I would love to see Terry and Flora give you what you're due, my granddaughter must be freed from distractions."

Hope shook her head. "It's my birthday, grandfather. And I'd like our guests to join us at the tavern."

Caleb shrugged. "We're a free nation. But they'll be paying for their own meals."

Hope smiled. "I know he's not really here to do tricks for my entertainment, but if he knows about my mother, perhaps he can tell a story about her."

A knock at the door sounded without warning, and Caleb breathed a sigh of relief that he didn't have to respond. "Come in, please!"

Christopher stood up politely and Hope went to the door as a pair of visitors entered, a young lady with dark hair and skin and an elderly woman with gray hair. "Long time no see, birthday girl!" The young lady embraced Hope tightly, but they soon looked up to watch an unnatural silence pierced by a violent glare directed at Christopher. The older woman slowly stepped toward Christopher, twirling a cane in her hand as the Enchanter grew more unnerved.

He finally cringed as he attempted a greeting. "Flora, my dear, it has been far too-"

"Wasn't short enough for me!" The old woman slapped Christopher on the cheek. "Audiences don't stay if you vanish too long, wizard. I've had my full, and I don't want to see any more tricks from you."

The dark young lady promptly marched to the couch where Hope had sat, eagerly munching a cookie. "My mother versus a wizard, this I've got to see!"

The old woman shook her head. "See? Oh, nothing to see. I'm sure he'll be leaving before Terry arrives, right, Caleb?"

Manny tried to intervene. "Actually, Hope invited us to dinner."

The old woman turned to Caleb in disgust, then back to Christopher as a smirk enveloped her mouth. "How fortuitous. We do have a lot of catching up to do, and I'd love a captive audience."

Christopher's shoulders slumped. "Eh, perhaps it's best if we leave now-"

"Oh, but we already negotiated payment." Caleb winked slyly. "Unless you'd rather leave here without my manuscript."

Christopher bowed his head and took a deep breath. "You're too generous, Caleb. Too, too generous."

Another knock on the door sounded, and Hope cringed at Caleb. "On second thought, maybe I don't need you both there. You've probably had a long journey. Maybe you should leave before-"

"Hope? Caleb? Everything alright?" A visitor called through the door. "Hmm, maybe they're at the tavern already..."

"Ugh..." Hope rolled her eyes as she welcomed two new guests, another young lady with brown hair and what looked like her middle-aged mother. "Awe, are you still down about this morning?" The young lady embraced Hope tightly.

"No." The older woman's icy voice was directed at Christopher. "This man's presence is more than enough to upset anyone."

Christopher weakly waved his hand in greeting as the new woman slowly walked toward him. She glared at him for a moment before a violent lunge had to be strained by Flora.

"How could you leave us like that! You were supposed to be here, you ape! He'd be alive if you hadn't broken your promise!" She fought momentarily before breaking down in tears and allowing Flora to guide her to the couch.

Manny offered Hope a sympathetic smile, recognizing that her day had been ruined and she could not speak up at all. He wished he could put his arm around her, offering a show of comfort to make a better impression, but he soon cursed himself. *You just met*, he thought. *Yes, she's pretty, but what do I have to offer her?*

Caleb finally mustered enough strength to stand. "I can see we're all upset now, and I know I could have prevented this. I've always said that an empty stomach only amplifies distress. Today is a special day for my granddaughter, and we shouldn't make it any more bitter. So, for her sake, let's all come down, breathe the mountain air deeply, and head to the tavern. If we can't break bread together tonight, we won't resolve anything tomorrow."

"What would you like to drink, young lady?" Someone had to break the awkward silence surrounding the table; it might as well have been the bartender. "We have a lovely new import from the Toltec Federation that's all the rage in Yorkton. Sweet and earthy, mixed into milk, they call it cacao."

"Y-yes, I'll have that." Hope would have killed for anything to dull her nerves. The shock of watching a classmate publicly beaten that morning worked its way further and further into her spine, and she would give anything for a moment to herself to process it.

"Coming right up, young lady." The bartender moved on to the other members for their orders.

Lauren was the first to finally notice Hope's dismay. "You're still broken up about Gareth, aren't you? What they did to him, that was truly awful."

"What was that?" Lauren's tone drew the attention of her aunt and guardian, Terry. "Did someone get hurt at school?"

Varsha sighed. "Boy refused to say the pledge; they dragged him outside and beat him in front of the whole class."

Flora was livid. "How dare they disrupt your schooling! I'm going to clobber that headmaster first thing tomorrow morning!"

Terry was less combative. "Money means less and less these days, Flor. Fealty to the Roots Party and Society of Virtue are all that matter. We knew it would come to this one day."

Christopher appeared puzzled. "Is the infiltration really that bad? Lady Angela warned me that diplomacy had broken down, but even she seemed unaware that your nation had become so captive."

"It's those damn goblins." Varsha was pleased with the look of displeasure her adopted mother, Flora, showed at her use of profanity. "We're at war now. They say we must bind society together, or the monsters will take us."

Manny appeared defensive. "Well, not everyone. Greystone County is still governed by those who value freedom."

Flora laughed. "Maybe in the city, boy. Outside those walls, the rest of the county has fallen. Who are you anyway? Not sure why Christopher felt the need to bring a pet."

"Oh please, stop it!" Hope jumped from her chair and shouted at the top of her lungs. "This is supposed to be the happiest day of my year, and it's absolutely rotten! I don't know this wizard or his apprentice, and I don't care what he did to any of you. He's here because he knew my mother, and learning more about her is the only thing that will give me any peace."

Christopher winked as Hope sat down. "I have just the story, young lady."

Caleb shook his head. "No, you don't. You barely knew her. We're here to celebrate Hope, not worry her. In fact, while we're waiting for our meal to arrive, let's open her presents, shall we?"

Hope smirked. "Christopher can go first. Now, wizard, what heart-warming story about my mother do you have to tell?"

"She was an Enchantress." Christopher seemed to take pleasure in Hope's surprise at his revelation. "Several years younger than me. While stationed at Angela's Haven, she joined me and a cadre of Professors and Rangers to investigate a lair of monsters right here in Braddock."

Varsha was immediately enchanted. "Monsters! I thought the goblins were new to the hills. I've never seen anything scarier than a wolf out hunting!"

Christopher shook his head in surprise. "You hunt?"

Varsha raised her eyebrows proudly as she reached into her bodice and revealed a necklace with a wolf fang. "I'm going to be a constable someday, I've got to know what's in these woods."

Christopher raised an eyebrow. "A female constable? I'm surprised that Society allows that – if they're as powerful as you say."

A loud creak of the door to their private banquet hall was followed by the growl of a familiar constable. "Everything alright in here? It is a tavern, but I can't let a young girl yelling go unnoticed."

Caleb waved his hand. "It's alright, Constable Sana."

Hope smiled at the officer. "I've had a rough day, but I'm feeling better now. Thank you, ma'am." Hope, Lauren, and Varsha watched in awe as she nodded and left the room.

"Oh, don't look at us like we're peculiar." Varsha's admonition was followed by the sound of a foot slamming and Manny wincing. "She's the closest thing we have to a role model in this town."

"A... constable? Do you all want to be one?"

Lauren laughed. "Hardly. She's strong, independent, commanding... everything opposite of what the *Feminine Virtues* teaches.

Hope smiled. "Of course, now that I know my mother was an Enchantress who fought monsters, I might aspire to something greater. Christopher, please continue."

"Food's here!" A bartender held open the door, and chefs carted in trays of food. Hope's mouth watered as she espied platters of fried chicken, bacon mashed potatoes, green beans with bacon, and coleslaw. The bartender placed a steaming drink at her place before any of the food was served, and she sat back and slowly slipped what immediately became her new favorite beverage.

Varsha laughed at her expression. "I already know I'm ordering a second round of that!"

Hope finally found herself able to relax as the chefs took care to plate the meal for everyone. Good food and a new drink would be generously topped off by a rare tale of her mother, information that her grandfather had always greedily withheld. It never sat well with her or her two best friends, orphans nearly from birth but kept ignorant of their true heritage. They had learned long ago not to question what came before, assured that they would only be upset by tragic stories, but that excuse held less power the older they became. Finally, in Christopher, she had someone who had no reservations about revealing her past, and she would do all she could to get every possible story out of him.

"Alright, Enchanter, tell me about my mother and the monsters." Hope sat back after a few bits of food and waited for Christopher to regale them.

"Ah, yes, fighting monsters with Gina Defoe." Christopher scratched his beard. "Was quite a long time ago, but I remember enough. About twenty years ago, Braddock was plagued by a den of Highlanders stealing children."

"Highlanders!" Varsha looked fearful for the first time in her life. "Those hairy red-eyed apes?"

Christopher nodded. "Crafty beasts, they called this world home long before we Skyborne arrived. Still bitter because they think we stole their world, thus why they steal children when they can."

Lauren's nose turned at the description. "And they use rotting animal carcasses as the plates for their meals. Despicable things. I'm glad the Haven got rid of them!"

Christopher shuddered. "How any of them have been civilized, I will never know. We knew the Highlanders near Braddock were monstrous, as half the children in the town had gone missing. They sent fifteen of us from the Haven to exterminate the monsters: five Enchanters, five Professors, and five Rangers. But something about it didn't feel quite right when we arrived. Gina found that our magic had vanished as our quest began. Sometimes, that is the will of the divine, and we leaned on the Professors and Rangers to discover the beasts.

"We finally found a child who escaped their clutches, but he seemed gripped with madness. Claimed that a human from the village had kidnapped them, only for the Highlanders to save them. It seemed improbable to us. Gina stayed in the town to investigate while we snuffed out the beasts. Not exactly protocol, but I wanted to see what she found.

"We finally discovered a network of tunnels on the cliffs nearby, and we freed as many of the children as we could before the monsters saw us. It took every constable in the village and every man who could wield a blade to light the tunnels aflame and clog the exits. We rid the hill country of their filth forever!"

Hope recoiled. "It sounds like the monsters weren't hurting anyone, though. What did my mother find?"

Christopher sighed. "It was true that a man had been kidnapping children, and Gina found him. The local tailor, as I recall. He would kidnap them at night, but the brigand claimed that the Highlanders always stole them away. Even tried taking a child from the school grounds in broad daylight. That's when several of the children were stolen away, and the Haven was called. A crowd of Highlanders revealed themselves and stole them from his grasp." The Enchanter finally stopped speaking, shuddering as he blankly stared at the plate of food below him.

Varsha broke the tension with a laugh. "That's not exactly dinner fare, wizard! Even my stomach is turning, and I regularly dress game that I've killed."

Hope found a reason to be happy. "This is the first lesson my mother ever taught me, Enchanter. That there are monsters in this world, but sometimes, people can be the true monsters. Thank you."

Lauren squinted at Christopher. "If that's true, why hasn't anyone here ever discussed it? A town like this would remember a tale like that."

Christopher chuckled. "Yes, I'm sure the Society of Virtue would love to remind everyone of a time when the Havens saved this village from a plague of monsters and an ignoble man. Allowing vivid contradictions of their precepts to proliferate should be rather high on their agenda."

Manny wiped his mouth and smiled. "Must be nice to hear something about your mother after all this time. Mine also died when I was young, shortly after my father and I immigrated to the Republic. I've had a couple of stepmothers since then, but neither even tried to take her place."

Hope was surprised to find a kindred spirit in someone from such a different background. "Do you remember her at all?"

Manny smiled. "Not as much as I would like, but enough to know she was a marvel. My father speaks of her often, like she still sits at our table each night. I think that's why he's been divorced twice. Nobody can replace her in his mind."

"Rotten luck for his wives." Varsha laughed and took another bite of her chicken. "Never thought I'd be this spoiled. Mother, I want you to invite a wizard who knew my parents for my birthday!"

"Are you... all orphans?" Manny appeared to immediately regret his insensitive question, quickly scooping mashed potatoes into his mouth.

"We don't talk about it. No use dwelling on that part of the past." Lauren nervously slurped her drink.

Manny sighed. "I'm sorry, that was rude of me. We've only just met."

Varsha laughed. "And we're unlikely to see you ever again. Not much of a point in getting to know you, is there?"

Hope avoided looking at Manny, worried that she'd give away a slight feeling of attraction. The young man was awkward, and she knew very little about him, but he was incredibly handsome, with high cheekbones, a svelte frame, and a small forehead. His eyes were brown like an oak tree, skin dark but lighter than Varsha's. She guessed he was from Castille, a land across the ocean that few ever left. It left the young man with a sense of mystery, a handsome stranger from a faraway land gracing her table... The Enchanter had given her two gifts today, a record for any one person.

The bartender soon arrived to interrupt her thoughts. "Pardon me, folks, the show's about to start. I'll open the shutters unless you prefer to continue dining."

"Ooh, yes please!" Hope was confident that the adults would start fighting again if they weren't given another distraction, and she wanted to get as much peace as she could before returning home. The shutters opened, and the banquet hall transformed into a balcony overlooking the tavern that doubled as the town hall, filled with half of Braddock's residents.

A band that had been playing finished their song as the stage was mounted by the innkeeper and Mayor, in office longer than Hope had been alive. Few outsiders had the opportunity to get to know everyone in a town like this, and preachers never stayed long enough to make an impression.

"Good evening, everyone. Just had a few announcements for you. Senator Polk wrote to me and said President Pilcher will assume control of the militia to go on the offensive against the goblins. Angela's Haven and the Empire have made it clear that we're on our own, so it's time to stop groveling and take the fight to the monsters!"

Most of the crowd cheered. "We all took a chance on President Pilcher a few years ago, a man who'd never served in government, and he was nobody's first choice – but by God, was he the best choice! There was no one better suited to guide us back to our founding values, and we needed an entrepreneur to truly unlock the potential of our own government. He'll take that same approach to the goblins and crush them just like he is crushing the recession and the moral deviance in the cities!"

Manny looked at Christopher in shock. "You have to say something! Aren't you here to help fight these goblins?"

Christopher sighed. "Certainly, but there's no use debating about it. This man has more goodwill with the audience than any Enchanter. We'll prove ourselves with our actions soon enough. There's no need to speak up now."

Manny shook his head. "Judge Craven tells my father all the time that speaking is the only way out of this political mess, that he only wins the election for Greystone Court by speaking to the people. Maybe the people of Braddock will listen to the son of their Sheriff-"

"No!" Christopher was firm. "You will learn in time that Enchanters are not interventionists. We only help the people who ask us for help. Give a speech as the son of the Sheriff if you must, but you'll lose your ticket to Angela's Haven. Leave politics to the politicians."

Manny appeared ready to respond but thought better and sat back in his chair.

Hope smiled. "I still think it's brave of you to want to say something."

Manny smiled. "Judge Craven likes to say that we're not descended from cowardly men. The only way to win is to fight in the first place. But I guess there's something to be said for choosing your battles. Judge Craven hasn't stayed in office for ten years by challenging everything the Roots Party does in Yorkton. He and my father plan for months before each election. I shouldn't be surprised that there's as much strategy to magic as there is to politics."

"Stop with the politics, you two. The best part's about to start!" Varsha punched Hope's arm and pointed to the stage as the Mayor gave his spot to Constable Sana.

Manny looked puzzled. "Law enforcement report?"

Varsha laughed. "No, silly! This constable is a thrill. She gets a little sloshed one night a week and tells a story about a historical event like she was there. Nursing dying people during the Iron Plague, defending civilians during the Massacre of Stalway, dueling with Jasmine the Wanderer... it's a real treat."

Lauren nodded. "And the musicians like it because it allows them to improvise."

Hope turned and concentrated on the stage as Sana took the stage, and the lights were dimmed. She was thankful for the darkness as she slightly turned her head and caught Manny staring at her, blushing in private. Perhaps, she thought, the words of *Madame Wanda's Feminine Virtues* would be fulfilled, and she would no longer have to worry about her future. "If a man comes upon you, rejoice! You've no further to look for a husband and can look to become his perfect wife. He will expect you to be supportive and obedient, and the

Feminine Virtues will guide you on the path to blissful matrimony..." No begging her grandfather to move to Yorkton only to share a room with her friends as they attended university, no shacking up with an uncouth logger, just an easy life as a wizard's consort.

"Godfrey, Richard, tonight we're going all the way back to the early days of the New Airgiallan Empire. That's right, whiskey, potatoes, and good old-fashioned... spying." Sana waited for the mass of harmonicas, banjos, and drums to eke out an Airgiallan melody, and she closed her eyes before reaching back into impossible memories to come up with a story.

"Once, during the reign of Empress Bridget, I was a soldier in the army of New Airgialla, stationed at Ballymalis on the west coast. As your history class may have taught you, Bridget was the first Empress to forsake the prophecies that Nikki's Heir would return. With the confidence of her lords, she ordered the siege of Doonagore, hoping that she could display a Deathlord's head on a pike at her palace in Armagh. However, my comrades and I were called to arms with a special duty: we were to infiltrate the fortress before the siege."

Once again, Sana inserted herself into the past, claiming to have joined an epic battle fought six hundred years prior. Snorts and giggles were barely muted by the slow bluegrass improvisations, and Hope began to feel sorry for the constable, worried that perhaps too much alcohol had cemented the delusion that she really had lived through all of these events.

"We donned armor stolen from the goblins that would conceal the whole of our bodies, and we took to the forest, joining roving bands of the creatures in pairs. Within a week, my company had found its place within the fortress of Doonagore, and our hearts bled at the depravity we witnessed. There is no law among the goblins, save the fear that compels them to obey their Deathlord and the other spirits haunting them. We were called to partake in wretched vices, and our bellies starved without clean water and fresh food.

"The worst part was knowing that we were doomed to failure. Whenever I saw one of my comrades resist temptation, I knew their victory would be rewarded with the execution destined for everyone who marched on the fortress. Only the Heir of Nikki could conquer the fortress, no matter how many soldiers Empress Bridget thought to send. As humans, we came to fight bereft of proper weapons, and as the day of war approached, we prayed that God would have mercy enough to save a few of us.

"By the time Bridget arrived with her army, my comrades and I had surveyed Doonagore and knew all of its weaknesses. Absent lousy luck, we could open all the gates, empty the parapets of archers, and allow our army to flow inward, cleansing the region of the goblin stain. But bad luck rules Doonagore, in the form of the Deathlord who dwells in dark dungeons below, seeing all who enter his domain and holding power over them. When the banners of New Airgialla appeared in the distance, and trumpets of war sounded, almost all of my comrades found themselves frozen in place and struck with crippling pain.

"Within moments, they were ravaged by goblins and the other foul beasts within the fortress, and the men who gathered outside the moat to begin their assault were assailed with missiles they did not expect. Arrows were followed by boulders from catapults, and as the army fled, the Gates of Doonagore were opened, allowing goblins without number to flood the fields, cascading the weeds with blood by evening.

"None of my comrades lived to see the light of day in their homeland, and it is only by the grace of God that I could remove myself from the fortress and fight my way out of the battle. When I got to the nearby woods, I forsook my garrison at Ballymalis and ran as hard as possible in the opposite direction. As the daze of battle left me, I took to my senses and obtained passage to the Republic, where I decided to become a constable. And thus I have served, in city after city, upholding the laws of the land."

Hope and her friends clapped as more locals mounted the stage, a group of older women performing a customary dance.

Manny snorted. "Funny well to talk about history. None of that's made it into a history book. What's the point of making up a story like that? It's not like there are even survivors who need comfort about their cousins dying in that fight."

Varsha rolled her eyes. "Oh, who cares? It's good fun and beats the propaganda they feed us at school. Opposing the narrative earns a beating from a constable."

A shocked Manny jumped from his chair. "My father would never allow that!"

Flora took a break from muttering with the other adults to laugh. "Your father never comes this far into the Hill Country, Manny Alonso. Yes, Christopher told me who you are. And if there's any bravery in your heart, you'll get up on that stage and strike the fear of God into them on your father's behalf!"

Christopher shook his head once more. "Don't make a scene, Manny. We're here for one purpose. Again, you can be an example of a leader to follow or watch your commands scatter like seeds on rocky ground."

Manny slumped back. "Becoming an Enchanter is really going to take some getting used to."

Varsha seemed content to follow her mother's lead. "A real man would go down there and stand for what is right. After all, Hope favored that boy who got beaten today-"

"Strike you!" Hope dropped her mug on the ground and immediately looked down, scared of the judgment that would condemn her temper. "I'm sorry, I need to... get some fresh air..." Standing up to leave the room, she waved away concerns from her friends and passed by an annoyed bartender on her way downstairs.

The dance drew to a close, and the Mayor would soon announce the last call so that constables could begin collecting drunks for the night. She made her way close to the front of the hall, keeping to the side so that no one would notice. Sixteen years had passed since her mother brought her into this world, and Hope had no idea what the next sixteen would look like. None of it was what she wanted – cleaning dishes in Yorkton, changing diapers at home while her husband got drunk, waiting on a husband... none of it was what she wanted. But none of it could be escaped unless she spoke up and said no to those erstwhile eventualities. Waiting for a man to come upon her as the *Feminine Virtues* prescribed was not an option – she shivered as she watched a maid in the corner bat away unwanted attention from a drunk while her boss ignored her pleas for help. Hope realized that is exactly what the *Feminine Virtues* intended for her, not to be swept off her feet by a caring gentleman.

"Excuse me, is there a copy of the *Feminine Virtues* in your guest library I can read to the crowd from?" Hope offered a young bartender a wide smile.

"Um... odd choice for music night, but I can't say no to a smile like that." He winked and vanished into a side room before returning with a dusty old copy.

"Looks like none of your visitors read this. It must not be a very virtuous establishment." Hope watered down the bartender's scowl by batting her eyelashes. Opening up to the passage on romance, she waited for the dancers to finish, then took the stage with the Mayor's permission."

"If a man comes upon you, rejoice! You've no further to look for a husband and can look to become his perfect wife. He will expect you to be supportive and obedient, and the *Feminine Virtues* will guide you on the path to blissful matrimony..." Hope read the words with reverence before angrily ripping out the pages and throwing them on the floor. Adrenaline surged as she was met with gasps and angry shouts.

"Those words used to mean something. But today, I saw it was all meaningless! I'm sixteen today, still in school, past the age many of you think your daughters should take a man. But today, I saw that being a man and standing up for your family means being publicly beaten by the headmaster. This is not the life I want for myself. This is not the life any of us want for ourselves. And when my generation takes over, we will burn every copy of this damned book!"

She smiled defiantly and felt empowered for the first time in her life, as though a stage preaching revolution was where she belonged. Looking to her left, she saw her entire dinner party rushing to the stage only to collide with constables ordered to disrupt the display.

Varsha was the first to beat the rush, and she picked up the fallen book only to tear out pages and throw it to the floor as well. "I don't know what's gotten into you, but I like it. Lauren, get up here!"

Lauren nervously ascended the stage and nervously picked up the book, but she seemed compelled to do the same as Hope and Varsha encouraged her.

"Alright, girls, this has gone far enough! You're not spending the night at home." Constable Sana wrapped her arms around them, and they struggled for a moment before glares from their parents told them to stop struggling.

Sana led them out of the tavern and down the street to the jail, and they said nothing to each other until they arrived. Expectations that they would be held together in a cell were dashed when Sana locked them in different rooms. Hope's room had a desk and a high-up window with an entrance to a cellar in the corner. She tried to open it to look for something comfortable but found it locked, so she bunched up her skirt and lay her head on it, thankful that she had worn warm leggings.

She wrapped her arms across her chest and shivered in the late winter air, desperate for a blanket. Eventually, she began to fall asleep, eyes remaining open as fatigue paralyzed her frame. She jolted upright at the sight of a pair of glowing red eyes in the window, but they vanished just as quickly. Be at peace, she told herself. Be at peace...

She began thinking about the story of her mother the Enchanter told, and she imagined that her mother was still out there, driving away the monsters. Yes, her mother was just outside, waving a sword and shield at the goblins creeping through the trees. Her bedroom door was reeking open as her mother snuck in to say goodnight, placing a hand on her leg… Her leg!

Hope screamed at the sight of the cellar door agape with a hairy arm reaching for her shin. She kicked at the arm but was not strong enough to deter whatever nightmare had grabbed ahold of her. Another arm appeared and dragged her forward, her head slamming into the door as she finally lost consciousness.

Chapter 3: Unwelcome Legends

Fear. It was all Hope could feel the moment she awoke upon a mass of furs. She was terrified to open her eyes, confident she would see an army of bright red pupils around her. If a monster had taken her, she had little time before it had its way with her, and she could either open her eyes now or have them wrenched open when the beast got bored.

Hope slowly squinted and found herself in a small cave that appeared to branch from a tunnel alit with firelight. Opening her eyes all the way, Hope sighed in relief to find herself alone. That would last just a moment, she was sure. The monster took precisely the right person – Varsha would have put up a fight, and if the beast had managed to drag her to its lair, she always had a knife on her dress to even the odds. Even Lauren, with her obsessive bibliomania, would have read something about how to best escape being kidnapped. Hope didn't even have her full skirt…

Her head shook quickly as she saw her lower dress splayed out on a rock next to her, a mystifying gesture from a mindless monster. But it would have been a wonderful gesture from a rescuer – the thought gave Hope relief momentarily, and she shifted her feet off the side of the bed to procure the garment. A moment later, the fear returned as her foot clattered against something metal that echoed across the cave.

"You awake. Good." Started by a gravelly, inhuman voice, Hope reached down and grabbed whatever she had kicked and found the ornate handle of a dagger in a leather sheath. Her hands shook as she fumbled the blade out of the holster and pointed it towards the door.

"Come out now. You safe." The voice stretched out every word slowly in between long breaths. Perhaps the speaker was sick… or maybe a monster simply did not have what it took to speak human words.

"My way out. One way." Hope scanned her surroundings once more and realized that there was, in fact, only one way forward. She could wait until the thing came to her or until a search party decided to venture into the caves west of town. This seemed terribly unlikely as she recalled the last time the constables and militia chased goblins into the caverns. The only survivor had been Lauren's late uncle Daniel, mortally wounded just so he could tell the tale.

"I know how to use this!" Hope knew immediately that her threat was unconvincing. Her voice was as shaky as her fingers, and in her haste to seem threatening, she did not process the fact that the monster might not even be aware that she had a weapon.

"No drink tea with knife. Drink with cup." That response merely stupefied Hope, and she let her hands rest at her sides while she considered the words. A monster's tea party was the stuff of dreams, and if this were real life, the *Feminine Virtues* would dictate that she be presentable. She nervously put the knife back in its sheath and stood up to dress herself with her skirt, tucking the knife by her waist so that her captor would not see it.

Slowly walking across the cave, Hope took a deep breath and peered around the corner. Her hand immediately covered a whimper from her mouth as she espied the unpleasant sight of a hideous ape-like creature with a scaly face hunched over a bubbling cauldron. It was a Highlander, the nightmare from legend rendered more horrifying because it was covered in an apron rather than in blood.

"What your word?" The Highlander struggled with each word as it waved Hope forward.

She peered at it quizzically and said nothing as it repeated itself. The Highlander shrugged and ladled tea into some worn clay mugs, likely stolen from town ages ago. It carefully set one on a flat boulder near the cauldron and took its own before sitting on the ground against another rock, wheezing for a few moments before taking a sip and sighing.

"Tea hot. Tea hot. No cold tea. Drink tea hot." The Highlander appeared annoyed that Hope was keeping her distance, and she slowly walked toward the cup for fear of antagonizing it.

She took a sip and made a show of smiling, surprised that a monster could have crafted something so delicious. It was a simple brew that made her feel relaxed and warm, and for a moment, she allowed herself to release the tension in her shoulders.

"What... your... word?" The Highlander coughed painfully as it spoke.

Hope raised an eyebrow. "My word?"

The Highlander huffed. "Your... word. Your... sound. Your... mother... call... you..."

Hope shivered as she realized what the Highlander wanted. "My mother called me Hope."

The Highlander laughed. "Hope! Mother... wanted... you... good... life..." Laughing appeared too much for the creature as it descended into a coughing fit and slumped back again.

I could just run. The thought crossed Hope's mind momentarily before she thought of the stories she had heard about these beasts. These monsters were feared more than goblins, driven to mortal rage when dying. If this Highlander was as ill as it seemed, it could go berserk if Hope tried to leave.

Hope scratched her brow. "Are you sick? I... I know a wizard. He can heal you."

The Highlander's eyes flared red. "No wizard! I... die... soon..."

Run, it's your only option. Hope could not know how to escape these caverns, but she would have better luck against something that could not breathe. Of course, if it caught her, there would be no way for her grandfather to find her body, and Hope could not do that to her grandfather.

She smiled intently at the Highlander. "What did your mother call you?"

The Highlander mustered something close to a smile and relaxed. "My mother called me Buline. She... wanted cubs... survive poison world..."

Hope shook. "Poisoned?" She was momentarily worried that Christopher's Haven force had poisoned the Highlander's brood. It struck her that she suddenly empathized with a monster just by learning its name – and despite the fear that had consumed her earlier, she felt at ease with the Highlander. No, Buline. She would call her by her name.

Hope took a deep breath. "Buline, who poisoned your caves?"

Buline cocked her head and squinted. "Caves? No. Poisoned world." Likely sensing Hope's confusion, the Highlander continued. "World belong us. Caves belong us. World poisoned. Now only caves belong us."

The words poisoned everything Hope had learned in the *Feminine Virtues*. She was taught that the Skyborne came to their world to tame monsters, but she had never stopped to consider that these monsters could feel pain. Especially after the funeral held for the men who had been slain by goblins, butchered in their prime without a care. Monsters had to be tamed for men to live. But if a Highlander could wear clothes and brew tea, why were they poisoned?

Hope felt a rare tie to her grandfather, ostensibly a historian who rarely discussed the topic with her. "Were you there?"

Buline's head shook. "I not there. I not mother's many years. Poison stole years. She more years than sky beasts."

Hope's spine shivered at the thought of a Highlander thinking her a monster. "We're not all beasts. I've... I've never met one of your kind before. And now that I know you have this lovely tea, well, perhaps I can visit again."

This made the Highlander smile. "You better other sky beasts. Sky beasts kill. Naked beasts. Shining beasts. Ground beasts. Shadow beasts. All hunt us."

Humans, elves, dwarfs, goblins... The first three had "tamed" the Highlanders, but the last were supposed to have been their allies. And – well, and Hope was supposed to rejoice when a man came upon her. The *Feminine Virtues* were dishonest from the first page to the last.

"I die today." The Highlander's mood shifted sorrowfully. "You have power. You use power good."

Hope raised her eyebrow, then let it fall, realizing that her expressions likely meant nothing to Buline. "What power?"

"Knife." Buline raised her arm and pointed a shaking claw. "In cave. Knife yours. Knife said you."

"But I don't have-" There was no point hiding the weapon. "Sorry, the knife next to the furs?" She put down her cup and slowly took the knife from her waist, gently lying it on her lap. "What do you mean by power?"

Buline sighed deeply. "Not knife. Power. Power lives. Power speaks. Power smells death. Power calls out. Power needs home. Power says you."

Hope suddenly felt uneasy, and the knife seemed to take on a heavier weight. She could have sworn it was making an impression on her skirt, and she quickly moved it to the floor. "It's just a knife." She was telling herself that just as much as the Highlander, worried her precarious situation made her vulnerable to Buline's superstitions.

Buline motioned for Hope to pick up the knife. "Knife yours. Take knife. Use knife good. You good, Hope. Use knife good."

Hope worried once more about risking the beast's rage. "If I take it, may I leave?"

Buline nodded. "Sky not far. Big tunnel." She pointed towards the noticeably largest of three different tunnels leaving the cavern.

Shrugging, Hope grabbed the knife and stood up, walking over to Buline. She awkwardly patted the Highlander's hair and barely avoided jumping away when the monster wrapped its arm around her leg affectionately.

Hope smiled. "Thank you for the tea. And… thank you for the power. I will use it for good." She bowed her head and ambled to the tunnel, then quickened her pace sharply once the cavern was out of sight. Still uneasy about the knife, she put it on the ground and continued walking briskly through the tunnel. Expecting darkness, she was relieved that her path was lit by glowing fungi on the ground and walls.

As she neared the sun, her expected sense of freedom began to turn to fear. Her hair began to stand on end, and she eventually froze in place. Slowly turning her head, Hope gasped at the sight of Buline squatting on the ground, red eyes blazing.

"You... take... power!" Buline's eyes shone brighter than the fungi, horns sprang from her head and fangs from her jaw as she tossed the knife at Hope's feet. The Highlander looked like it was about to lunge, and Hope sprang down to grab it before running as fast as she could into the forest's fresh air.

After running as fast and far as she could, Hope doubled over and panted heavily, ambivalent to whether the Highlander had followed and was about to attack. She was far too fatigued to fight back, even with the aid of a knife. The Highlander looked like it was one step away from jamming it between Hope's ribs so that she would keep it.

"Hope! Christopher, I think that's her!" The voice of the Enchanter's apprentice Manny was not the one Hope needed to hear, but any human was better than a monster.

"Hello!" Hope could barely speak as she cried out from depleted lungs.

The Enchanter awkwardly embraced Hope when he and Manny arrived, but she did not reciprocate. It was an odd choice for a man she did not know whom her grandfather seemed to intensely dislike.

Christopher sensed her indifference and quickly backed away. "The whole town is looking for you. Your grandfather is a wreck! We'll all be pleased once you're back home."

Hope cringed. "They don't think I ran away, do they? I don't want to go back into a locked room."

Manny shook his head. "On the contrary, they found signs of forced entry and a secret tunnel dug into the Constabulary. Everyone assumes you've been kidnapped by goblins. The militia is being called up to find you!"

For the first time that day, Hope felt true relief. "Well, they can be called off. I'm home in time for dinner. Just take me to my grandfather's so I can rest."

Christopher suddenly tensed up as he saw the knife in Hope's hand. "Did you find that Dagger in the caverns? Was there a witch? Hope, you need to tell me everything about that."

Hope blinked and offered it to the Enchanter. "Would you like it? I don't think I'll ever need a weapon like this."

Christopher's recoil puzzled both Hope and Manny. "No, you keep it for now. But I must know what manner of witch kidnapped you, young lady. That's no ordinary dagger."

Hope pursed her lips as she tucked the Dagger into her waist again. "Not without my grandfather. Please, just take me home."

The Enchanter frowned. "If that's what it takes… In fact, it's best if this journey is silent." He snuck a worried glance at Manny, and Hope began to fear for her safety. If this Enchanter suspected something evil, he could revisit it on a young woman without consequence. As directed, they said nothing other than a brief conversation with a constable in town to announce Hope's rescue.

A joyful embrace from her sobbing grandfather ultimately changed the mood once Hope finished the short journey to her home. Manny was dispatched to alert the Constabulary and Hope's friends. Hope was brought to the couch before a roaring fire and a platter of cookies with coffee.

Her grandfather's hand affectionately rubbed across her knee as his mood transitioned to absolute joy. "You have no idea how worried I was, darling. And no idea how happy I am to see you back!"

"Don't get too happy." Christopher's dour words were met with laughter.

"Oh, save the debriefing for later. This isn't a Haven mission. My granddaughter is home, and she can tell us what happened to her once she's had a proper nap." He enthusiastically grabbed a cookie and began munching until it dropped onto the ground. "Hope... what is that? In your dress?"

The look of revulsion on her grandfather's face terrified Hope. "I don't know..." She realized quickly that he wanted more. "It's a knife. See?" She pulled it from her waist and offered it to her grandfather, who merely scooted away.

"Christopher." Her grandfather stared intently at the Enchanter. "Grab my talisman treatise from the shelf and turn to page 78. And... you..." The lack of familiarity in his voice was disturbing. "I want to see the blade."

Hope nervously withdrew the Dagger from its sheath and was dismayed to watch her grandfather grow more worried. Christopher finally thumbed to the page in the book, studying it for a moment before looking at the Dagger, his gasp masked by the thud of the tome hitting the floor.

"What in the name of the world is that doing in your hands?" Her grandfather's tone changed as he saw the fear in Hope's eyes. If he thought she was a monster at first, he now seemed to think she was in danger.

Christopher uneasily brandished his staff. "Caleb, it's a simple matter to tell whether she is bewitched. A talisman like that doesn't just come into someone's possession."

Caleb shook his head. "She's been through enough. Let her tell her story without fear. I lost her mother and her grandmother. I don't want to lose my granddaughter to hysteria."

Christopher remained uneasy. "Speak. If there's a witch in your head, just know that this will be unpleasant."

Hope took a deep breath. "Something took me in the night. I hit my head, and I don't remember what happened after. I awoke in a cavern with..." She took another deep breath, her heart rate rising. "There was a Highlander, it gave me this knife."

Christopher smirked. "Impossible, witch! I killed the Highlanders here long ago!" He lifted his staff but cautiously put it down when Caleb glared at him. "Well, maybe one escaped. But a mindless beast has no need for such a weapon."

Hope shook her head. "Its name was Buline."

Christopher rolled his eyes. "For a witch, you're not very convincing. Highlanders taking names?   In the wild? You're on the wrong side of the continent to find a civilized Highlander!"

Hope shrank back as her grandfather held up his hand. "I believe her, Christopher." His words took the Enchanter aback. "I know, I know, now you think I'm being bewitched. But I know my granddaughter, wizard. And if you let the fear go, your spirit of discernment will say the same."

Christopher sighed and closed his eyes, lips moving as he mouthed deep thoughts. Finally, he shrugged and relaxed. "Turns out I could have used your wisdom just as well these long years, old friend. She is telling the truth. No witch, just a monster."

Hope sighed audibly and placed the knife on the table. She scooted left and hugged her grandfather, a tear running down her cheek as she received his embrace in return.

The tenderness of the moment was lost on Christopher. "But you know just as well as I how much danger she is in. We must get her to Angela's Haven at once! In fact, all of you-"

"No." Caleb shook his head. "The three girls need to leave, yes. But we will need to stay here. I'll let you take that treatise with you, because I won't need it. That apprentice of yours is fetching Flora and Terry, right?"

Christopher nodded. "They better be ready. Just a thought, though – you don't expect they will allow me to take them to the Haven alone, do you?"

Caleb shook his head. "Nor will the law. You'll have to bring a constable. Probably the one who arrested them last night, Sana. Not sure how there's a woman in the Constabulary in times like this, but we're blessed."

Christopher made his way toward the couch and knelt before Hope. "I am sorry for judging you, young lady. As long as I've lived with my gift, I should have known you were in trouble and not an enemy. Moments like these humble the greatest of Enchanters."

Hope dried the tears on her cheek. "Thank you, Enchanter. I… I know you meant nothing by it. The Highlander called it a power, and that made me worry. I should have expected it would worry you, too. In fact, I tried to leave it, but the Highlander was most insistent…"

Christopher stood up and went to pick the book off the ground. "I don't blame you. And I don't blame even a monster for trying to get rid of the Dagger."

A knock on the door sounded, and Flora, Varsha, Terry, and Lauren hurried into the house, her friends jump on the couch to embrace her.

"How many goblins did you kill to escape?" Varsha laughed as she looked at the strange knife on the table.

Lauren rolled her eyes. "Relax, don't make her think about monsters."

More tears rolled down Hope's eyes as she hugged her friends tightly. "I barely understand what just happened. I'm just glad to be home… for now…" Her eyes darted towards Flora, who was eyeing the knife with the same apprehension Christopher and her grandfather had shown. Caleb shot Flora an understanding nod, and her expression morphed into terror.

Manny hurried down the main avenue and went to the Constabulary, where peace officers finally rested after a busy morning.

"Is Constable Sana here?" His question was immediately met with the Constable's appearance. "Um… Mr., um… Defoe, I think his name is? You need to come to his house. The Wiz-uh, Enchanter, I'm with, he says you need to escort a party to Angela's Haven."

Sana laughed. "Sure, just tell him where to send the bill first! You believe this wizard, boys?" She summoned the laughter of her comrades. "Sorry, boy, we don't take orders from the Haven. Get the Sheriff of Greystone to send a letter, then we'll consider it."

Manny smirked. "That can be done. But I think my father would be far more interested to hear that a young woman who needed his Constable's help said no in her hour of need."

The constables in the room froze before one laughed. "Almost fell for that one! Sana, lock him up for impersonation!"

Sana chuckled dryly before studying Manny's face intently. "Now that I think about it, I remember seeing a kid with Sheriff Alonso at our last evaluation in the city. And he's dark like the Sheriff, too. So I'll wager you, boy. When we stop in Greystone on the way to the Haven, we will visit the Sheriff first. And if he don't recognize you, I'll drag you right back here to rot in a cell. Maybe even throw you to the goblins that struck last night!"

Manny was angered by Sana's disrespect, but he quickly decided that restraint was more becoming of his father's station. "He'll be more than pleased by your due diligence, Constable. Perhaps he'd authorize a promotion to Inspector."

Sana pursed her lips. "Don't get too elaborate with your stories, kid. That's when they start to fall apart."

Another constable shook his head. "You're not seriously going, are you? Who exactly needs to be escorted out? Wait, wait, don't tell me – it's those girls, isn't it! Probably a witch that put them up to being disruptive last night! Well, tell the wizard s to exorcise them extra good! We let it spread, that's how the goblins win!"

Sana withdrew her cutlass. "Hmm, looks sharp enough, I'll need a whetstone just in case."

"And a change of clothes, don't want anyone thinking we're working with the Havens again." Another constable winked. "He's a peculiar sort of wizard himself, so that'll make it extra weird."

Sana glared. "I earned this uniform, and I'll wear it with honor. Besides, bandits who see a constable on a road will think twice about attacking. Now, when do we leave, boy?"

Manny shrugged. "I assume first light, since getting to the main highway takes a day."

Sana nodded. "I'll be ready."

Manny took his leave, pushing away thoughts of asking for a Constable's uniform himself. The profession was not inherited, but as the son of the Sheriff, it would not be too ungainly for him to dawn the brown tricorn hat, blue coat, and velvet trousers. It might also give his father the wrong idea about his desired profession.

Upon returning to Hope's home, he found the mood somber, exhausted occupants stewing in their anxiety. Caleb's eyes were puffy, his beard wet with tears, while Flora and Terry appeared equally upset.

Christopher had shed no tears but was still burdened by what Hope had found. "What did the Constable say?"

Manny tried to lend some certainty to the situation. "She'll join us. Sana, I mean. Told her who my father was, she'll be ready to go with us at first light tomorrow."

"Does he know?" Flora was more angry than sad.

Manny shook his head. "I'm in the dark. Hope found something, didn't she? Something terrible?"

Christopher nodded. "Her grandfather will explain it to her later. She found exactly what we came to find, Manny. A talisman. Likely the source of the goblin raids."

Caleb nodded. "You'll read all about it later. A talisman bonds to its host. When the host dies, the talisman calls out to the spirits around it. Demands to be found. A map of the raids will likely reveal that they center around Braddock. This talisman must be taken to Angela's Haven before it bonds with

Hope swiftly. Because this particular talisman has a habit of drawing dragons when it changes hands."

Manny gasped. "We have to go now! We can't outrun dragons!"

Christopher waved his hand. "Don't be so worried. We have the advantage over them where it counts. We'll keep that secret for now. Hikaru has a small army with him at the inn, and they will be more than enough protection for the two days it takes to get to Greystone from there."

Manny shrugged. "Well, you're the Enchanter. Are... are they ok?" He nodded toward the hallway.

"We'll take care of our children tonight." Flora stood up. "Leaving still needs to be their choice, but we know which choice they'll make. Girls!" Hope, Lauren, and Varsha quickly filed into the parlor. "Varsha, we're leaving for the night. The three of you have a long journey ahead of you tomorrow." The three girls were mystified and anxiously left after offering Hope their valedictions.

Christopher and Manny took their leave, heading toward the inn for a room the Enchanter had booked the night before. "Need a drink, young man?"

Manny peered curiously at the wizard as they entered the tavern. "I'm seventeen."

The Enchanter shrugged. "Best to be sober at a time like this. We need clear heads, even when our hearts seek relief." He approached the bar and dropped four large gold coins. "Two mugs of tea, cream if you would."

A bartender initially looked annoyed, but his eyes popped at the size of the coins on his bar. "I could give you both our largest steins of cacao for that! And still make money!"

Christopher smiled. "If you would. Keep the change, it's just weighing down my horse."

The bartender speedily prepared the drinks, and Manny and Christopher took the mugs to their room. Christopher pensively sipped his beverage while Manny heartily sipped his, expecting comforts to be few and far between before they returned to Greystone.

Christopher finally paused and looked at Manny on the bed opposite his own. "Remember when I said we were on the cusp of an adventure?"

Manny nodded.

"I was wrong. Far from an adventure… The cusp of a new epoch in history. What Hope found was no ordinary talisman. There are many, many different types found all across the world, some benign, some good even." Christopher paused and took a deeper sip. "This is not one of them. What Hope found, improbably, is the talisman of a Deathlord…"

Manny's eyes popped. "A Deathlord! Which one?"

Christopher's shoulders shrank into a defeated sigh. "*The* Deathlord, my boy. The Locust. That it's here rewrites nearly a thousand years of history. You know the legend that the Airgiallan Empress Nikki sank that demon's talisman into the ocean?"

Manny nodded, thirst vanishing as he stared into a suddenly unappetizing mug. "She didn't really, did she?"

"Caleb has a scrap from one of the first printings of *Jasmine the Wanderer*. It says when the warrior was present at the death of Nikki, the Empress ordered it strapped to a wild boar and released into the wilderness. Somehow, she believed it could be used for good, to keep the remaining Deathlords at bay, if the right person found it. There's far more to tell, but that's more or less how it ended up here. I'm surprised that a Highlander received it without drawing attention, and Caleb himself may not even know. We must be thankful we found it in time to leave it in Angela's hands." He eyed his mug wearily before finishing his drink.

Manny also decided to finish his drink, secretly ashamed that he was more excited than terrified by the road ahead. Noble motivations were necessary for him to become a legend himself.

"One more thing." Christopher began to remove his cumbersome robe before bed. "Don't tell Hope. She knows she has a talisman and that it needs to get to Angela. But knowing what is in her possession, well, it's too great a burden for someone like her to bear."

Manny nodded. This was not about him. But he was here for a reason, and if he could do some good by protecting Hope from this perilous knowledge, it would be a solid first step on his road to becoming an Enchanter.

"Tell me about my mother." As Hope and her friends embarked on their journey early in the morning, she thought back to the night before when her grandfather finally told her a story about her mother. Heading into the unknown with just her two friends and a few adults she did not know, Hope had to bind herself to the familiar. She was not built for adventure.

Caleb's demeanor had immediately soured at his granddaughter's demand the night before. Still, he seemed to realize that little else would calm her. She had told Lauren and Varsha what befell her in the Highlander lair. While they were sympathetic, they were as uneasy as Christopher had been at the sight of the talisman. Her mother was the only one who could love her unconditionally as her spirit wandered the afterlife.

Stroking his snow-white beard, her grandfather had agreed. "Alright then, Hope. Gina was a spirited woman with a strong temper. I'm surprised that my blood was strong enough to make you a calm person, thinking of the tantrums she used to throw! What a child she was..." His eyes glossed over, and he paused, burdened by some terrible memory of his own daughter's life.

"She finished school a year early and joined the New Airgiallan Navy, of all things." Her grandfather seemed more amused than anything at the thought. "I forbade her to fight, but she pushed me aside, and there, I believe, she met your father. He was a nice man, but when they returned to our town from fighting in the North Sea, I wasn't originally able to get along with him. Thankfully, he loved your mother as much as I, so we were able to bond-"

"You've told me most of this before." Hope frowned, and she saw her grandfather taken aback by her irritation. "But what of my mother? Her temper? What was that like? You never told me that she was so spirited."

Her grandfather relented. "Your mother was quite clever, but as that silly book for girls says, wisdom is for men. Your mother's reputation as a ringleader in school was deemed a threat at one point. She and a few other girls in town were invited to Yorkton to meet with the Chief First Secretary of the Society of Virtue, ostensibly to be honored but secretly to be chastised. When your mother was made to trade her trousers and knife for a dress and a pen during the meeting, she sensed dishonesty and schemed to teach the leader of the Society a lesson.

"The night before the meeting, she snuck out of the inn where they were lodged and found a vagrant sleeping in an alley. She informed the fellow that she would meet with the Society of Virtue the next morning, and she paid him part of the small stipend she had been offered for recognition. In return, he would make a show of attacking the Society leader in the street during their meeting the next morning. When she and the other girls had finished breakfast, they marched down the street to the Hall of Virtue, meeting the Chief First Secretary outside. The vagrant arrived and began pulling off wigs and grabbing at dresses until your mother threw off her dress to reveal her old hunting clothes. She made her own show of beating the fellow senseless to prove her worth beyond the mandates of the Society. Oh, she got in quite a bit of trouble for causing such a fright to those women, but I was proud that she stuck to her true nature."

Hope had smiled and chuckled throughout the story, feeling more warmth within her soul than any coffee or fire could ever muster. That warmth would be her only shield against the chilly mountain air, baring some sort of enchantment. She shivered, less because of the late winter air and more because the memories of a dream crept into her head. There was an impression of a dragon, some ravenous monster that descended from the heavens and burnt Braddock to ashes.

She had never felt much affinity for this drab town where trees grew tall and trees never took root. But everyone there was a person just like her who deserved a chance at life. It was tempting to dwell on the thought that her discovery had brought something evil upon the town. Still, she quickly remembered that she was taking the Dagger away. The power, as the Highlander had called it, would be contained at Angela's Haven, and she could return to her life of obscurity. Justice in this world was a matter best left to the wizards.

"Hope." Lauren's words were the first to pierce the calmness of the forest. "Varsha and I wanted to say we're sorry if we made you uncomfortable last night. You've always been there for us. We're always going to be here for you."

Hope was relieved by the genuine smiles on their faces. "Awe, that means the world. Nobody could ask for better friends dealing with something like this."

"What exactly is this, again?" Constable Sana's intrusion was most unwelcome.

Christopher jumped in before Hope and her friends could bungle a cover story. "They're suffering from, eh… latent possession. It's a complicated enchantment, likely from one of the witches that the Haven suspects is controlling the goblin attacks. Stray to close when a spell is cast during a walk in the woods, you might get cursed without knowing it! Terribly tragic malady. But easily remedied by a skilled exorcist."

Sana frowned. "Not something in your bag of tricks, is it?"

Christopher shook his head. "My gift is in discernment. It took my eye to tell that they had a problem, and under my watchful eye, we will shield others from being infected. They don't truly know themselves anyway at this age, and with demons coming back and forth, it's only a matter of time before the darkness takes hold."

Sana remained suspicious. "Why wasn't the constabulary told about this? It's not like the Society to keep such information from us."

All eyes were on Christopher as he prepared to make or break the journey. "They didn't know what they were dealing with. Young Miss Lauren's mother tried to speak to the Society here, but they were dismissive. She wrote to the Society in Greystone, who contacted the Haven Cathedral. I was already due to visit the hill country to investigate the goblin attacks, and it was requested that I take a look."

Sana shrugged, mostly satisfied. "Odd for a wizard from Byeong's Haven to be in the hill country."

"Constable, his title is Enchanter!" Manny's outburst was jarring. "My father demands that all his officers treat people respectfully."

"Wizards." Sana rolled her eyes and started muttering to herself as she prompted her horse to trot forward. "Not half as powerful as they claim, not half as helpful as they could be…"

Varsha laughed. "That took some guts, learn that from your daddy?"

Manny frowned. "Treating people respectfully is a universal value. If the law doesn't treat people respectfully, why should we respect the law?"

Hope winced at the memory of Gareth's beating two days prior. "The law only respects the wealthy these days."

Manny appeared shocked. "Don't tell me you've witnessed bribery in your village!"

Hope could not help feeling disheartened by his reduction. "A boy was dragged from school and beaten yesterday because he refused to say the oath of loyalty to the Republic. The headmaster said he had to beat him because his father is dead… and unmarried widows who can't even work in a town like this are being taxed in exchange for their care."

This quickly summoned Christopher's ire. "Was there no preacher to call your village to charity?"

Varsha laughed aloud. "Preacher? Ha! The Haven church was closed a year ago, the Mayor's son turned the inn into one of those Free Churches aligned with the Roots Party. The only preachers are the ones who want to travel this far out of their way on a weekend for pitiful tithes."

"Shush!" Lauren surreptitiously nodded in Sana's direction. "We can't say these things."

Sana turned her head back at the party and smirked directly at Lauren, who cringed and awaited chastisement. "Relax, children. I'm only here to arrest real criminals. Don't kill, don't steal, don't breach the peace... But curse the Roots Party all you want, they mean nothing to me."

Lauren's fear quickly turned to relief. "That was... close."

Christopher looked solemn. "You'll need to keep everyone you hold dear secret. Until we reach the Haven, speak to no one. Don't say your names. Don't say where you're from or where you're going. Don't pull your coins from your purse. This road will only grow more treacherous, and my mission is to ensure this doesn't become a tragedy."

The Enchanter's words uncomfortably ruminated in Hope's mind as she anticipated the perilous road ahead. Every newspaper claimed there were goblins around every corner in the hill country, and she suspected it had something to do with the Dagger in her possession. If it was as terrible as the Highlander claimed, it would draw dark things out of every hole and crevice wherever she went. An odd peace crept in when she absent-mindedly grabbed the hilt. Perhaps she could defend herself with this legendary power if it came to it, no matter how unwelcome it was.

Chapter 4: Unwelcome Goblins

There were moments when Hikaru wished he was still surrounded by bodies willing to throw themselves at the enemy. Fewer now that he was a diplomat, but when the time came to draw the sword against monsters, bandits, and hostile powers, the expendable soldier was the best tool in his arsenal. While there were many skilled fighters in his caravan of fifty resting at the Inn, every single one was the son of some noble favourite or proud Peer in the Imperial Diet, and he could not blindly risk their mortality.

"When do we strike?" A young cousin of the speaker of the Diet named Taro knew better than to utter a single word. The goblins they tracked had no unique sense of hearing, but Hikaru feared a witch more than this piddling war party.

Hikaru merely turned and glared at his companion in the trees, watching the goblins below. A party of five had come out of their hiding place to practice archery, firing wooden arrows from crude bows drawn by silken strings. These monsters had struck before, but they knew little about the value of their spoils, mistaking finery for functionality.

The sound of a rabbit running nearby caused one goblin to turn from its practice and stare toward the blind where Hikaru and Taro were perched. Taro broke a branch as he recoiled at the sight of the beast, but he thankfully drew no special attention. He had likely never seen one in person, learning about the monsters from books and paintings. Nobody ever forgot their first vision of a goblin, short, gangly creatures with bulbous heads shaped like upside-down tears and eyes as black as a starless sky. Stare too long in that void, it was said, and that void would drag you into the realm of demons.

"When do we strike?" Taro spoke out of fear this time. The youthful desire for glorious battle was gone – and it was precisely what Hikaru needed. To deliver the blow to these creatures, he required someone focused on living to see the next day rather than living on as a legend.

Hikaru nodded and closed his eyes, reaching out his hands as he focused on his memories of the monsters below. He focused on their greenish-gray skin, calling forth boils on their torsos beneath the rags and metal scraps they used as an excuse for armor. Opening his eyes, he watched as the goblins below slowly began to drop their bows and reach inside their garments, irritation eventually transitioning to pain.

Four of them were soon writhing on the ground, wholly disrobed and howling at the sight of blue spots on their chests sprouting into lime-green blotches. The one goblin Hikaru had left undisturbed tried to pop one of the lesions with an immaculate constable's sword it had stolen, only for its comrade to scream so loudly that the nearby birds immediately flew away. As the four stricken goblins slowly found their chests melted by boils, the one survivor hurriedly backed toward a tree and witlessly swung its cutlass around.

This was the sign Hikaru needed. "One arrow."

Taro was confused. "It'll take more than that to kill-"

"One arrow." Hikaru was adamant. "I don't want it dead. Did you mislead me about your skill with the bow?"

Taro nervously looked down at the longbow in his hands. "I will not fail you, Minister." A moment later, the goblin was felled by an arrow through its knee.

Hikaru and Taro cautiously jumped from the tree and drew swords as they approached the goblin, thankful their ears could drown out harsh noises. The goblin tried to crawl away but finally lay as still as possible with Taro's sword at his throat.

"Name the witch." Hikaru began using the common tongue of Manifest, guessing that the goblin knew enough to understand it. When the goblin simply looked to the ground, Hikaru repeated himself. "Name the witch."

"Should I finish it?" Taro smirked at the dying creature below him.

"Goblin." Hikaru was pleased that the monster at least recognized this word, looking up at him intently. "Name the witch. You will be healed."

This made the goblin more frantic, and as it remained silent, Taro raised his sword in the air. "You will be my first kill, bakemono!"

"No witch!" The goblin screeched as loudly as it could. "We obey Skurlag."

Hikaru raised an eyebrow and scratched the stubble on his chin. "Skurlag. Who is this... Skurlag?"

"We bow to Skurlag. By Skurlag, we will be one." The goblin remained fearful as the glint from Taro's sword vanished into its obsidian eyes.

Hikaru realized how little he knew about the goblins in Manifest. "Is that your word for the Locust?"

"The Locust!" It was the one joyful-sounding word the goblin could muster. "The Locust will make us one! Skurlag says we are close!"

Hikaru looked up at Taro and winked for him to prepare his kill. "Close?"

"Yes, close, close, close!" The goblin's new euphoria was disturbing. "You can feel it, can't you? It draws near!"

"Wait." Hikaru motioned for Taro to drop his sword. Closing his eyes, Hikaru quieted his ears and sensed for the darkness in his surroundings. He was near the main road from the Inn to Braddock, a brazen place for increasingly militant goblins to train. He could feel something dark approaching as he shut out the physical world.

"Kill it, quickly." Hikaru smiled at the goblin as he delivered his orders in the tongue of Nara. He stared directly into its eyes as Taro delivered an instant, unexpected blow.

"We must fortify the Inn. Something dark approaches." Hikaru sheathed his sword and began hurrying toward the road, wishing he had a horse. As he calmed his senses and reached out into the spiritual realm, he could feel it getting closer, and he realized that he and Taro would not make it to the Inn together.

Hikaru stood in the middle of the road when they reached the highway, solemnly drawing his sword. "Go back to the Inn without me. Warn the delegation that a witch approaches."

"No!" Taro drew his own sword. "I will waylay them. Her majesty cannot afford to lose you."

Hikaru shook his head and placed his hand on Taro's shoulder. "Nobody else in that Inn has but a spark of magic. I can kill a witch, but not the goblins she would summon. If you warn the others, you can prepare them to hold the Inn. Stay with me, and innocent blood will be shed. Go!"

Taro appeared relieved as Hikaru sent him on his way, free from the fear of an immediate death in the wilderness. Hikaru's retinue and the well-armed merchants at the Inn would more than sufficiently hold back the small force of goblins in the hills. According to the Republic's reports, there would be a couple hundred of the creatures at most. Easy work for a squadron of warriors hand-picked from the Empress' personal guard.

He hid in the trees alongside the road and looked west, eventually surprised to see six people riding horseback. As they drew closer, he realized that one of them wore the orange robe and red sash of an Enchanter from Byeong's Haven, and he worried that somehow Christopher had fallen only for his form to be possessed. The caravan was odd for an assembly of witches and warlocks. Christopher was deep in conversation with Manny, his young acolyte. There were three teenage girls, one deathly somber opposite two chattering incessantly. Improbably, the column was tailed by a rare woman Constable who appeared more irritable than evil.

Hikaru decided to take a chance for his friend's sake, and he quietly stepped into the road while announcing himself by loudly drawing his sword from its sheath. "Christopher, if you've been possessed, I'm giving you one chance to be set free."

Christopher turned in shock, but his eyes lit up in relief, and he jumped from his horse to run toward his old friend, only for an embrace to be rejected. "I know why you're wary of me, old friend. Manny, lead my horse. Hikaru and I will walk the rest of the way. It's not far."

Hikaru remained wary as he sheathed his sword and walked by Christopher's side, the distance between them and the horses growing. "You know I sense something evil among your party."

Christopher nodded. "The worst Enchanter in the world could sense it. I went to Braddock to find information about talismans. Instead, the granddaughter of an old friend found one."

Hikaru stood still, eyes widening. "A Deathlord's talisman? So that is what is calling the goblins out of the dirt. Tell me – do you recall any goblin name for a Deathlord that sounded like Skurlag?"

Christopher scratched his beard. "No, but their speech is not exactly an elective at the Haven. I would not be surprised to learn that it is their name for the Locust."

"The Locust will make us one." Hikaru's delivery of the goblin's quote made Christophe shudder. "I went hunting while you were away. I killed a few before I found you. One of them said that they would become one by something called Skurlag. I asked if that was their word for the Locust, and they said the Locust would make them one."

Christopher sighed. "They still remember the demon that gave them command over the world. Those poor, tortured souls. We may yet put them out of their misery. Keep walking, old friend. We'll need to get our rest. I'll need you to escort me to Angela's Haven quicker than the wind."

Hikaru nodded and began moving. "I will do whatever you ask. If you found a Deathlord's talisman, only Angela can keep it safe."

Christopher nodded. "I tell you this in confidence, old friend. My apprentice knows, in case I do not survive the journey. The talisman that the young lady found is *the* talisman. You know to whom it belongs. And you know that dragons and every other manner of foul beast will come for it shortly."

Hikaru anxiously squeezed the hilt of his sword. "I will not fail you."

Manny was thankful that he would spend the day riding in a wagon rather than on horseback. He hated ending the days sore and bow-legged, and for the time being, he could rest and focus on listening rather than riding. Following the journey from Braddock to the highway, a good night's sleep had left all of Manny's companions in good spirits. Hope was quiet but cheerful, Lauren and Varsha chattered cordially, and even Constable Sana appeared personable.

Christopher had tasked him with surreptitiously observing Hope that day, curious if the talisman had started to influence her. So far, Christopher had only shared the nature of the Dagger with Manny and Hikaru, mandating that the secret be kept until they arrived in Angela's Haven. Even there, Christopher wished it could be handed off to Angela without incident, Hope returning to her life none the wiser. All she and her friends would know is that she had found a talisman, and that talisman needed to be led away before it called out to monsters and dark magicians for help.

"The air is so much warmer down here." Varsha was the first to break the silence as they set off in the wagons that transported Hikaru's diplomatic retinue. "It'll practically feel like spring in Greystone!"

"It'll stay warm for a bit. Just long enough to enjoy the best part of our journey." Manny winked. "We're stopping at the Inn at Dead Falls tonight. Not many lovers slink away to the hot springs this time of year."

Lauren was ecstatic. "Hot springs! Oh, that sounds lovely! Much better than dousing one's body with tepid water."

Hikaru's assistant, Yukio, seemed less pleased. "Why do they call it Dead Falls?"

Sana smirked. "An old ritual. Years ago, monsters and witches would kidnap people, tie them up, and throw them from the top into the great pool below. The shores were lined with fire so any survivor would burn upon escape." Yukio shuddered, but Sana winked. "Don't worry, it's all gone now. Like the boy said, lovers slink away here when they wish to be alone."

Yukio shook her head. "You dishonor the lost by making it a place of celebration. It should be solemn, the home of a shrine. Turning a graveyard into a temple of entertainment is dishonorable."

Manny shook his head. "The matter came before the Greystone Court years ago. Judge Craven spoke most eloquently on the matter. We make Dead Falls a place of celebration precisely to rebuke those who sought to spoil nature."

Varsha chuckled. "You really are a politician's son. Why in the name of the world do you wish to be an Enchanter?"

"Probably politics." Lauren shrugged when Manny tried to shake his head in disagreement. "Greystone is the last county under the control of the Branch Party. Judge Craven is the only leader with the stature to run against President Pilcher next year. Suppose his own Sheriff's son is enrolled as an Enchanter. In that case, it will make him a more legitimate alternative to those who support the Havens."

Yukio nodded in concurrence. "The politics in Yorkton are not favorable, Manny. A Senator was just forced to resign because he did not disclose his divorce twenty years ago."

Sana's smile turned to rage. "How dare you malign our Sheriff! His personal life is no concern to anyone, least of all the Empire of Nara. How he conducts himself matters only to him and his family."

Manny nodded in approval. "Many thanks, Constable. My father prizes loyalty."

Sana's frown receded. "I will admit that I'm surprised to see you enroll at the Haven rather than the Constabulary, but I trust your father's wisdom. He is the only bulwark for the law's defense against politics in this county."

Varsha snorted. "Politics is what has kept the Sheriff from doing something about these damn goblins! There's a reason why he has to take command of the militia. Even if you heard them howling at night as far away as Greystone, you have a giant stone wall to protect you. We have nothing up here."

Lauren's breath began to audibly quicken. "Strike me, can we stop the wagon? I need to clear my head."

Yukio shook her head. "We can't afford to stop, Minister Hikaru says nothing can delay our journey to the Haven. Are you sick?"

Varsha rolled her eyes and put her arm across Lauren's shoulder. "Her uncle was killed by goblins last year, elf. This always upsets her."

Manny was horrified by the course of the conversation, saddened that Lauren's nerves were collapsing. It was worrying that Sana knew more about his life plans than his own father, and he would have to work hard to keep her from revealing his secret. What was more troubling to him was the blind eye people saw his father showing towards the hill country. Lauren's pain was not his father's fault, but perhaps her sacrifice could be a remedy."

Manny took a deep breath, knowing he was revealing secrets to a foreign diplomat encaged by a vow of secrecy. "The President has barred our requests for aid."

Sana recoiled. "What requests? The Inspector and the Mayor both say they had to appeal to our Senator for help because national defense is the Republic's responsibility."

Manny nodded. "A responsibility that the President refused to accept when he ignored repeated requests from Greystone for better weapons and training. My father and the Judge knew it would make the President more popular, but they didn't care! They had too many widows scream for aid. They brought those appeals to the President, and he did nothing until it was too late. I was shocked when your Mayor said the President was to command a militia he had abandoned. There's a reason why your Uncle died, Lauren. And it wasn't my father."

A silence fell over the wagon's inhabitants. Yukio took a notebook from the pocket of her dress and began taking notes, a consequence that would bring his father a great deal of grief. For now, he hoped it would bring some closure to the distressed young woman in front of him.

The awkward silence was finally broken by Hope. "Yukio, tell us about your country."

It was not the result Manny sought, but at least there would be peace in the wagon once more.

Yukio sat back and tapped her pen on her notebook. "No place in the Hemisphere surpasses the Islands of Nara in beauty. It is a land where all are at peace, in harmony with a perfectly balanced nature. We take what we need, but no more. We give all we can and receive much in return. You look to the sky and see birds, we gaze into the clouds and see dragons-"

"Dragons!" Manny chuckled at the way the word was repeated. Varsha was intrigued, while Hope and Lauren were shocked.

Yukio simply laughed. "There are many different kinds of dragons in this world. The dragons that soar across the deserts of Cimarron to the west are the monsters that you know, as are the beasts that scour beneath the ground of Karelia. The balance in Nara I spoke of extends to all creatures, even the dragons. We give them space and freedom. Many farmers offer them livestock, and in return, they keep the fields free of predators."

Expressions of fear remained in Hope and Lauren, but Varsha remained intrigued. "Tell me about your dragon."

Yukio's head shook. "How did you know?"

Varsha smiled. "Your hands are callused, and not just from writing. And your face has seen a great deal of sun, just like Sana. Now tell me about your dragon."

Yukio sat back and peacefully looked at the ceiling. "I called her Raiju. I grew up on a remote island farm. Raiju protected our fields, but we kept our distance from the creature. They are fearsome in the distance, with blue scales blinding in sunlight, wings bringing tempests, and claws shredding all they touch. But my parents assured us that this dragon was trustworthy. As long as it was fed, it protected us. It could not be known, like people know each other, but it followed patterns."

Varsha was entranced. "So it could be trained, like a dog?"

Yukio nodded. "But better. They are clever, like cats. When I was a maiden, the islands were attacked. Goblin ships under the command of dark magicians began to raid Nara's outlying islands. We lived far inland on the largest isle, but they only saw it as more of a prize. The farm was attacked, and the monsters chased me away through the nearby forest. I was pursued, and I thought perhaps the dragon might think the goblins a meal and protect me like it protected the farm.

"I ran to the caves in the hills where I knew my dragon lived. Raiju heard my screams as the goblins arrived, and she let loose a deafening roar. The goblins thought she was one of theirs, and they stood still when she swooped down to feast on their flesh. When we were alone, the dragon let me spend the night in her cave before flying me back to the farm the next day. Raiju kept returning but would not leave after its meal until I came and patted her on the nose."

By the end of Yukio's tale, even Hope and Lauren were as enthralled as Varsha. Manny's anxiety about their danger receded as he wondered whether the Dagger could command a dragon or a goblin. Perhaps Hope could wield it to keep them safe... Or maybe a great Enchanter could use it to defeat the Deathlords once and for all, freeing the Hemisphere and allowing the world to become one. The talisman seemed beyond redemption, but so did dragons, and here was an example of one of these creatures bonding with a human because of something more than food.

Varsha broke the peace once more. "You seem awfully fixated, buddy." She nodded toward Hope, who turned away a blushing face that had been in Manny's direct line of sight. "Found something you want to take home from your journey already?"

Lauren elbowed Varsha sharply. "How dare you! So soon after... you know. It's not right. I'm sure Manny knows to mind his manners."

The color drained from Manny's face. "I meant no offense, there's a lot on my mind. I've never been surrounded by so many elves before, and I'm so new to this enchanting business... My mind was prone to wander."

Varsha smirked. "Oh, so you don't find Hope attractive? Odd for an eye that so often wanders her direction like yours."

Manny cringed. "You're plenty beautiful! It's just that-" He stopped for a moment, saddened that Hope's look of curiosity started to recede towards disappointment. "My father raised me to focus on the mission at hand. To put aside distractions, no matter how... intriguing."

Varsha continued smirking. "And what exactly do you find intriguing about Hope?"

Manny thought quickly. "She ought to be asking questions like this, don't you think?"

Hope hung her head in embarrassment for a moment, then raised it once more, her eyes appearing to flash. "Alright, Manny. What do you find intriguing about me?"

This wasn't the reaction Manny expected. "Well... oh, strike me, all of you! I'm here to study enchantments, not romance. I don't know you well enough to have any sort of feelings about you. It wouldn't make sense, would it?"

Varsha clapped her hands. "How about a game? You two ask each other questions. If Lauren and I like your answer, you can ask the next one. If not, we'll let the other ask. And since Manny seems so alone out here, let's have him go first."

Manny gulped as Hope batted her eyelashes. "What's your favorite book?"

Hope was quick. "Easy, *Jasmine the Wanderer*! Now, that's the kind of powerful woman we all aspire to be."

Manny smiled. "I've read it several times myself, she crossed paths with many interesting people. Jasmine herself doesn't come across as particularly..." He struggled to find the right word in a space full of women staring intently at him. "Agreeable."

Hope scrunched her nose. "That's what most men tell me. And I think that's because of how men often see women. Disagreeable, irritable. We open those pages and see a woman reacting normally to arrogance and greed. In contrast, the boys see themselves acting the way they're taught. There's a reason that it's still so popular in schools."

Lauren appeared shocked. "That's not what you wrote in your essay! I wrote that in my first draft, and you told me to throw it away so I didn't get in trouble!"

Hope looked down. "I'm sorry. I should have been more bold. It's how I really felt, and I shouldn't have pushed my fears on you. I just feel a little bit better about speaking my mind today."

Sana finally interjected with a laugh. "Maybe that's why your parents think you're possessed! You're just being yourselves, and that's becoming a crime."

Varsha frowned. "Stop it, everyone, this is supposed to be a conversation between Hope and Manny." Everyone nodded, and she smiled proudly at her restored power.

Manny smiled wide at Hope in keeping with the game, then became stoic when she blushed. "My favorite book is *The Hostel of Schmidt*. It's a marvelous collection of Thuringian folktales. I love the framing, a lonely man offering a home to pilgrims for the night in exchange for stories. It shows people from all walks of life shielding themselves from magic and monsters with morals and faith." He added the last part, believing it might buy him some goodwill with the women surrounding him.

Varsha shook her head. "Bit dull for my liking. I think our Hope deserves a man with more exciting tastes."

Lauren nodded. "I think it's a fine book, but there are few translations that make it compelling. Hope you're up now!"

Hope thought for a moment. "What do you find attractive in a woman?"

Manny's heart began to pound, and he could think of nothing that would not end in stuttering. If he described her, it would be too obvious. If he described someone completely different, it would drive her away. The latter would probably be the wisest approach, as he could not be sure he would ever see Hope again after the journey. But if their paths did cross again…

"A kind heart." Manny let himself speak without settling on anything in particular, and he regretted his lack of eloquence. "I mean – my father always imparted this to me. It doesn't matter who you are or what you do with your life. It matters how you treat people. And besides, everyone needs someone to be their conscience. My father says that Judge Craven calls him the angel on his shoulder, keeping his more combative impulses at bay. I want to serve people around me and be with someone as fully dedicated as I am to the cause of the downtrodden and destitute, just like our faith decrees." He wished desperately that Hope would find his words profound rather than meek.

Hope shrugged. "I'm looking for muscles." She chuckled as Lauren and Varsha laughed aloud, all equally entertained by the despair that consumed Manny's face before he realized it was a joke.

Hope reached her foot across the wagon and tapped Manny's boot. "I want someone who makes me laugh. But more importantly, I want someone who will stand by me whatever I seek to do in life. And who wants me to do more than raise children. I don't know what that is, and I've never been allowed to wonder. But now that we're on the road, bound for a magical city, I feel the possibilities are endless. And that's what I want a man to offer me."

Manny said nothing, merely staring intensely into Hope's eyes. Hope seemed uncertain initially but soon stared back just as intensely as they thought about their prospects. Hope knew little about Manny, but she could surmise that becoming an Enchanter rather than a constable like his father likely generated friction. And now he knew that she was

unhappy with her life, seeking something completely
different.

Sana's scoffing finally tore their eyes apart. "If this
whole trip's going to be like this, that exorcism won't come
soon enough!"

Hope was exhausted by the time the wagon train
arrived at Dead Falls Inn. Emotionally, more than anything.
She adored the company of her friends, and she was enjoying
Manny's attention far more than she would admit. But she
found herself relying increasingly on a sense of independence
that came from the talisman in her possession.

This ornate Dagger hanging from her belt was
something that both a monster and a powerful Enchanter
feared. It made her grandfather weep, yet it left Hope with a
sense of power over the people around her. Thankfully, this
dreadful thing would be removed from her soon enough, but
she almost felt she would miss the talisman once it was gone.
She even felt that it would miss her, too, but that was too
bizarre a fantasy to be true.

Upon their arrival at the Inn, Hope and her friends
exited the wagon with Sana and Yukio. Christopher and Hikaru
were the only other travelers to enter the establishment, and as
Hikaru secured rooms and meals, Christopher called Hope
aside.

The Enchanter nervously gripped her grandfather's
book about talismans. "Hope, this Inn is not that well
protected. We will likely survive the evening, but if goblins
should attack, we will find this particular tavern difficult to
defend. You must keep the Dagger with you at all times. Do
not let it stray from your care. But most importantly, you must
not use it to take a life. If we are attacked, there will be plenty
of people to protect you. This talisman may seem like an
ordinary knife, but taking a life will unlock a dark enchantment
that can destroy your soul. Promise me, for your grandfather's

sake, that you won't use it as a weapon under any circumstances."

Hope nodded, unnerved by the Enchanter's own anxiety. "He left me in your care. If you say that I shouldn't use it, then I won't."

Christopher smiled weakly, barely relieved. "You'll be sequestered to your rooms for the night. Sad to say you'll miss the hot springs out back, but they haven't even built a wall, and you can't risk it." He was quick to chase away the grimace from Hope's face. "You and your friends will feast tonight, I'm taking care that you'll see every other comfort they can offer. Your grandfather doesn't wish for you to attend this journey wrapped in despair."

Hope bowed her head. "You're too kind. Don't worry about us."

She joined Lauren and Varsha on a journey upstairs, where they were led into a divinely furnished room with two beds. Lauren and Varsha put their bags on one bed, and Hope thanked them for their consideration. This journey was dangerous for all of them, but she was thankful that they recognized the burden she bore carrying a talisman.

No sooner had they unpacked than a knock sounded on the door, readily answered by Varsha. "Ready for a soak in the hot springs? My treat!"

Lauren beamed, but Hope shook her head. "Christopher said no. He wants us to stay inside because of the goblins."

"Goblins?" The maid at the door laughed. "We are perfectly safe! They haven't come this far down the highway. Besides, we keep several seasoned hunters on the payroll to scout the woods for threats. If goblins were anywhere near here, we'd know."

Varsha smiled. "See, there's no problem! But if you want to be extra safe, we can invite Sana and Yukio. I'm sure Christopher would be fine if we're protected by a constable."

Hope nervously grabbed the hilt of the Dagger but quickly found herself thrilled by the risk. "You're right, I'm exhausted! A hot spring would do me some good. Sana, too, by the looks of her. Um... will I be allowed to keep my dress nearby?"

The maid raised an eyebrow. "There's a closet near the pools, but... well, if you want it resting on the ground next to you, that's your business. Shall I fetch your fellow travelers?"

Varsha nodded. "They're next door. But, uh... let's go first, then invite them down." The maid shrugged and invited them to follow.

The hot springs were segregated in the name of propriety. Hope and her friends were given light garments that kept them more than decent. The maid led them out back to a series of pools overlooking the majestic Dead Falls and the river below. A large wooden wall separated them from the pools occupied by male travelers, and the young women were able to settle into the water peacefully. Only a couple of other pools were occupied, enjoyed by women of various ages. Acclimating to the water proved elusive, as their peace was soon interrupted by Sana and Yukio dressed in their traveling clothes.

Sana was particularly unamused. "You three are supposed to be in your rooms! This is no place for you to be with goblins around. And don't think you can tempt me to join you. There are stringent laws against bribery, and if I jumped in, I'd be fit for a prison cell!"

Yukio was equally apprehensive. "The code is the same for Nara's diplomats. We need our rest. We won't stop tomorrow until we reach Greystone."

Varsha rolled her eyes and sat back, arms resting behind her head. "Up to you. This is just how I'd prefer to rest. Do what you want."

Hope and Lauren stared awkwardly but suddenly winced and covered their ears at the sound of horns and howls in the distance. Looking up, they were horrified to see dark figures line the river shores with torches. They pointed madly toward the sky only to see more dark figures with fire at the top of the waterfalls gather. The howling reached a rhythmic crescendo and was suddenly hushed, only to be followed by terrified cries from people thrown into the falls.

"Inside, now!" Sana withdrew her cutlass and pointed toward the Inn as the establishment immediately turned into a frenzy.

Hope and her friends bounded towards the Inn, Sana in tow, when Hope realized she had forgotten her dress by the pool. She turned and ran, sidestepping an irritated Sana as she began to see goblins get closer to the pools. In her haste, she slipped on a puddle and tumbled headlong into a pool, her head bashing against the side as her thighs crashed into the ridges surrounding the pool. Weakly lifting herself up, Hope found herself pulled from the pool by a terrified Sana.

"Leave that stricken dress and run!" Sana's shout was soon accompanied by a groan as Hope struggled to stand. "You can't run, can you?"

Despair consumed Hope as she grabbed her crumpled dress and sat at the Constable's feet. "Take this and give it to Christopher."

Sana gritted her teeth and shook her head. "Curl up and put your hands over your head. I'll hold them as long as I can."

Hope followed Sana's orders and waited for the worst, her hand digging through her dress to grab the Dagger. Christopher's vague warning about not killing held no court as she envisioned getting in a couple good stabs before being bludgeoned to death.

The first of three goblins made it to the deck, howling at the sight of unprepared defenders. A more stout goblin with a fearsome club charged at Sana, who deftly sidestepped him and elegantly slid her blade into its back before kicking it into a pool.

"That all you got?" Her challenge was met by two shorter goblins with crude spears that rushed forward to meet similar fates. Just as Sana dispatched them, they drew the attention of a larger war party. "I'm so sorry." Sana's last words to Hope contained no expectation of survival.

As the monsters surrounded them, Hope finally grabbed hold of the Dagger and felt a much stronger connection to the enchantment inside. Ignoring Christopher's words, she opened her mind and listened for the Dagger's call. *Use me.* Hope's head briefly shook. *I can set you free.* Hope nodded and closed her eyes as she felt a strange tingling sensation behind her pupils. She weakly lifted herself up, pointing the Dagger towards them with trembling hands.

Sana swung her sword in front of Hope. "Get down!"

"Hahaha!" A goblin with an ornate broadsword laughed. "Let the little one fight! The monsters are here, little one! You can't just close the bedroom door! You can't just call for your mammy!"

The goblin sprang forward, and Hope tripped backward onto the ground, groaning first, then shrieking as the goblin fell atop her and let out a death cry. Looking up, she was horrified to see the Dagger's blade sticking out of its back, and she fearfully kicked the body away. *Perfect.*

The Dagger clenched Hope's hands around its hilt even more tightly, and she failed to resist its call to fight. Jumping up, she raised the weapon above her head, shrieked something unintelligible, and drove the Dagger through the heart of a goblin that was preparing to finish off Sana. A bright violet light shone forth from her eyes, casting a purple hue over the world.

Sana stepped back, eyes widening in disbelief at the power that suddenly coursed through Hope's body. The Dagger seemed to become one with Hope's hand, and she began cutting away at the enemies around her. Fighting through the shock, the goblins descended upon Hope and Sana once again, but an ancient wisdom guided her at every turn, telling her how and when to strike the foes that continuously circled the pair.

Time lost meaning as more and more goblins howled and joined the fray, only to fall to Hope's violet fury and Sana's blind aggression. Hope was vaguely aware that Christopher and Hikaru's warriors slowly fought their way to Hope's side as the battle went on, elves driving their swords through the corpses of survivors. Nothing could stop the killing – Hope had bonded with her weapon, and it knew exactly what needed to be done to keep its bearer alive. Every sword, every spear, every axe, and every blow delivered by an enemy was thrust back, usually ending in death until one very skilled opponent was left. Hope blocked each sword thrust and delivered some wounding slashes, sure that she would find her mark just as directed by the Dagger – her Dagger. Nothing would drown out its voice, overpowering her beyond the wild cries of her current foe. No matter; anyone who cried loud enough to drown the voice of the Dagger would quickly find themselves without their tongue –"

"Hope! This has gone far enough!" Christopher's voice hit Hope's ears like a thunderclap. Hope suddenly grew dizzy, dropping the Dagger and gazing in horror at the bloody cuts she had inflicted upon a weakened Sana.

"What have I done? What have I done? What have I done?" She repeated the question again and again, gazing up at a dark, starry sky until the world faded away.

Chapter 5: Unwelcome Refugees

Manny sat calmly with Christopher and Hikaru throughout the journey from Dead Falls to Greystone, listening intently but remaining silent as the two Enchanters plotted their best path forward. Sana's cries of indignation rang in Manny's ears like she was present in the wagon, even though she rode her own horse in solitary anger alongside Hikaru's wagon train, and communicated nothing. The constable knew something was wrong with Hope, and she raged at the Enchanter for what seemed like an hour before he could finally get in a word.

"Strike me, wizard! Actually, no, strike you! Strike every single one of you! Strike Angela's Haven and strike Angela! And when God is done striking you down, may he raise you up so I can have a go! What in the name of the world is possessing this girl?"

Christopher's teeth had chattered aloud, almost more because he was afraid of Sana than pumped full of adrenaline. "Sh-sh-she... She found a talisman. One that had an enchantment. She needs to be cleansed-"

Sana had spat on Christopher's robe. "Talisman? Enchantment? That's not how combat works! You don't just simply fight that many enemies without tiring. And it was barely a fight! It seemed like the goblins were just throwing themselves at her, begging to be impaled on that creepy little knife! She just drank it in with pleasure."

Manny had put his finger to his lips as Hikaru's mean put an unconscious Hope on a stretcher. "You'll wake her, she needs some peace after-"

"Oh, I can't wait to wake her!" Sana brandished her cutlass like she would strike Manny with the flat of her blade but thought better of it. "She's going to owe the entire military staff an explanation! And you'll give them one from a jail cell the moment we enter Greystone. What I just saw was no mere enchantment. That was the worst kind of dark magic at work.

Anyone who can command goblins and take that much joy out of dealing death is a witch, plain and simple."

"Oh, like you don't have secrets." Manny covered his mouth after forgetting his place, looking away from Sana's piercing glare.

"What kind of secrets, boy?" She cocked her arm on her waist and growled.

Manny had taken a deep breath. "You don't fight like an ordinary constable. I know, I've seen their training. In fact, you fought better than any soldier I've seen, from the Republic or anywhere else. Why's someone with your skill hiding in a tiny town like Braddock?"

Sana had frowned. "None of your concern, boy. But I'll make this whole mess your concern if you don't tell me what the wizard is really up to! Your father won't want his son consorting with witches, and if Judge Craven is half as close to the Sheriff as you describe, he'll recall your father himself!"

Christopher had sighed. "Oh, if you only knew, constable. Hope is in grave danger, her soul imperiled by something far more terrible than you could imagine. Greystone will not survive what is coming if you don't let her go to Angela's Haven immediately."

Sana had been wary of his statement, but remained unconvinced of his innocence. "You have exactly right now to tell me why I shouldn't shove you and Hope in the same dungeon, wizard!"

"She's possessed by the Dagger of the Locust!" Manny had believed Hope had no other option. Christopher had groaned in fear more than anger.

Sana had shaken her head. "Impossible. We all know that Empress Nikki had it thrown in the ocean."

Manny had straightened his posture. "You really want to lean on that after what you've seen? A 16-year-old girl just took down a force of 100 goblins by herself! No armor, no sword, no enchantments. Just a knife. How do you plan to explain that? I will face my father when we return and show him proof. He'll believe his own son."

Sana had finally settled. "I was still debating whether you were the Sheriff's kid, but I think I believe you after all. You'd only expect a parent to believe a tale this tall!" They had left it at that. Sana was appeased enough not to run away alone, even though she stayed silent. But her words would be crucial when they finally arrived and needed to prove to his father what had befallen them on the road.

The wagon train grew anxious when they finally approached the edge of the hill country and beheld the southern plains looking toward Greystone. Smoke rose from several points in the west that Manny knew were small towns, their occupants now thronging the roads leading to Greystone. A way out from the bottom of the hills, they found themselves in a massive line of refugees carefully guarded by beleaguered constables and militia.

Manny recognized a familiar face and called to the driver of his wagon. "Hey, call that constable over!"

A constable trotted over on horseback and gasped at the sight of Manny's face. "By the powers, Manny! Your daddy's had us looking for you the whole day! What in the name of the world are you doing with a bunch of elves?" Christopher poked his head out of the wagon to see what caused the commotion. "A wizard, too? Now, there's a story for the campfire!"

Manny's stomach soured as he realized he would face his father shortly without any preparation. "Constable Travis, it's a longer story than I can tell right now. Can you get the wagon train into the city? We need to speak with my father at once! And we have wounded."

Travis shrugged. "Kin or not, your daddy says no favoritism. Maybe I can let in one wagon, but if we these people see the whole train go by, they'll rush the gate, and ain't nobody getting in after that!"

Manny sighed. "If you can take one, that'll have to do. Are we under attack?"

Travis nodded. "Goblins have taken every city between Martingale and Greystone. Couple of dragons circling with them. They say there's some sort of witch controlling 'em. The Empire is pushing through from the west, but it'll be several days before they arrive. Every village has been abandoned."

Manny poked his head back inside the wagon. "The three of us can go into the wagon behind and get through to the front. My father won't let in the whole wagon train because he thinks it'll cause a riot. Will your retinue be fine without us, Minister?"

Hikaru frowned. "I need assurance that they will be allowed into the city. It's not your father who worries me, it's these jumpy boys with toy swords terrified of death."

Manny smiled, making his way to exit the wagon. "I can make certain." Leaving the wagon with Hikaru and Christopher in tow, he waved to Travis. "You need to post a guard to this wagon train and let everyone else know they are to be allowed in. Can you do that?"

Travis nodded and waved to an approaching militia man. "Major Curtis, keep these wagons under guard and make sure they get inside the city. They're friends of the Sheriff's son. Besides, we'll need every blade we can get."

Major Curtis peered down warily at Hikaru and shrank back when met with the elf's stoic expression. "Pointies better fight on the front line, we ain't got enough supplies for a siege!" Manny was tempted to respond but said nothing when Hikaru ignored the insult and walked into the next wagon over, Christopher following behind.

An excited call from Travis led Manny to stay outside the wagon. "Hey, you're that lady constable, right? From Braddock?"

Manny bid a chuckle as Sana rode to meet them. "Ain't you that boy constable from Greystone?"

Travis leered. "Watch your tongue, that ain't virtuous now, is it?"

Manny waved his hand. "Enough fighting, she protected us from a goblin attack, Travis."

Travis laughed, eyeing bandages on Sana's left arm and right leg. "More like she just barely survived! See, they got in a few good licks!"

Manny intervened quickly. "She fought a witch."

Travis was horrified. "The witch, I reckon? The one commanding all these goblins? She have long claws like they say?"

Sana smirked. "Longest you ever did see, deputy. The kind that wreck your ears when she drags them along the wall of your room at night, or cut up your feet in the dark when your mother hasn't tucked you in properly."

Travis gulped and tried to hide a fear Sana had ascertained. "Ugh, lady constables. It ain't right. Manny, you have that wagon follow me. You make sure this one keeps her distance. Might be the witch in disguise." Sana laughed at his misgivings while Manny re-entered the wagon.

Christopher put his finger to his lips as Manny entered the wagon, where Hope's haggard friends had been attending to her feverish and unconscious frame. "I told them what we know. Minister Hikaru will have them sheltered at his cousin's Hotel, and we can make our way to your father."

Manny nodded, mystified at the coincidence that the elf had a relative in town before snapping his fingers. "Of course, Hirose Hikaru!" He quieted his speech after Varsha glared. "Sorry. Minister, it's your family that owns those hotels?"

Hikaru nodded. "The vision of my grandmother, a taste of Nara in every great city the world over. Seldom found in any town so small as Greystone, but it was our first in the Republic. Nostalgia is... unique in our family."

Manny offered Lauren and Varsha a reassuring smile, reflecting on his many visits to the Greystone Hirose Hotel. It was the most extravagant building in the city by far, only shorter than the courthouse. Few chefs in Greystone offered better meals than the exquisite and plentiful Naran cuisine cooked daily. The more Greystone society felt chafed by the Republic, the more the elites patronized the establishment, daily filled with the wealthy and influential seeking fine food and noble culture.

The wagon passed the line of refugees into the city painlessly, peace only broken by the occasional jeer. Most people appeared far more terrified at goblins they had seen burn their homes than elves running from the same danger. Upon arrival at the Hirose Hotel, Hikaru had attendants escort Hope, her friends, and Yukio inside. Horses were procured from the stable for the elf, Christopher, and Manny, and they made their way alongside Sana to the Citadel, where they would meet his father.

As Manny expected, the Citadel was abuzz and heavily fortified. He led the party through the main gate and into the tower at the courtyard's center. True to form, Manny's father was in the center of it all, a tall presence warily looking out for the many men around him whose mothers he would have to inform of their deaths. The man wore his full suit of armor in a show of morale, bearing the burden his me would face on the walls inside a comfortable room where he was completely safe.

"Manny!" The sight of his son was the only thing that could interrupt his father's work. Manny smiled weakly as his father ran forward and embraced him tightly, armor knocking the breath out of him. "We need to talk right away, to my chamber."

Manny followed his father to an office, awkwardly leaving the party to fend for themselves. "Father, I need to tell me something-"

"Yes, you do!" The disappointment was stifling. "Father Jerome told me everything this morning. I just want to know one thing from you, young man." He took a deep breath. "Did I show you so much disregard that you felt you had to hide this from me?"

Manny cringed. "Father, I can barely believe that I have the gift of miracles! You're a man of the world. Focused. Firm. Magic seems a silly distraction from the life you live. I didn't expect the Enchanter who evaluated me to drag me on a quest so quickly."

His father sighed deeply. "I understand why you hesitated. Magic has not had a real home in our corner of the world for some time. It is alien to both of us. But I've tried, by God, I've tried, to make you feel like you're your own man, haven't I? Sure, I've talked to you your whole life about becoming a constable, but it was only supposed to be one option. I met countless aimless men who lacked a vision or a purpose, and all I tried to give you was something you knew you could do." He sighed again and opened his arms for an embrace.

Manny looked down and slowly accepted his father's embrace. "I'm sorry. I'm... I guess, well, maybe I'm afraid. This country isn't exactly friendly to Enchanters."

His father chuckled. "No, I suppose not. And neither am I, now that one stole you away! You could have died out in the hill country."

Manny laughed. "Well, I nearly did."

His father pulled back, face aghast. "Tell me everything."

Manny cringed. "That'll be hard, I feel like I've lived a lifetime in a few days. The Enchanter took me to Braddock, and we met an old friend of his along the way. Hirose Hikaru, Chief Minister of Nara to Manifest. Yes, the Hirose." He nodded as his father raised his brow in curiosity. "We went to Braddock to meet an old friend of his, a retired Professor who had a rare treatise on talismans. Apparently, Angela's Haven was concerned that a witch was controlling the goblins. Well...." He paused, preparing for the incredulity. "His old friend's granddaughter found a talisman while we visited. And in the book, he learned that when a talisman's host dies and changes hands, it calls out to the nearest monsters and dark magicians for a short time, seeking to be rescued."

His father nodded. "And do we know to whom this talisman belonged? If we return it, a dark magician might be convinced to abandon this invasion."

Manny pursed his lips. "I know, but I can't say. You saw the Enchanter who was with me, he can explain more."

His father shook his head. "I know you want to be an Enchanter, Manny. And you don't want to risk his anger. But you are a citizen of the Republic and, more importantly, my son. You need to tell me everything."

Manny huffed. "Look, it's bad enough that it needs to get to Angela's Haven immediately. I wish I didn't know. You'll wish you didn't know. What is it Judge Craven always says about deniability?"

A knock on the door interrupted them, and his father frowned. "You can ask him yourself. He's the only one who can disturb me." His father opened the door and stared quizzically as Judge Gunther Craven entered the room with Christopher, Hikaru, and Sana in tow.

Judge Craven looked as regal as ever, clad in dark flowing robes with an ornate rapier hanging from his belt, outfit only modified by carrying a spear rather than a staff. "You showed poor hospitality to your guests, Juan. Do you know who you've left waiting?" He nodded at Christopher."

"Christopher Deas, Governor of Magic at Byeong's Haven." The Enchanter bowed.

Manny's father raised an eyebrow. "You're a long way from home. As are you, Chief Minister Hirose."

Hikaru bowed. "At your service, Sheriff. My retinue is at your disposal, few though we are. I bring but fifty warriors."

Manny's father smiled. "Your Empress' aid is too kind. We can have them drill immediately. You may wish simply to observe, but your sword would be welcome." He turned to Sana. "And you. Constable... Sana... Freeman! The only woman in my constabulary, hard to forget. Anything to report from Braddock?"

Sana stared at Christopher and Manny before huffing. "Nothing you don't already know, if your son is good for his word. And nothing else that you want to know."

Judge Craven raised an eyebrow. "Deniability, smart. Guessing we don't want to know why exactly an army of goblins is outside? That all we have to do is kill them; leave the dark magic to Angela's Haven?"

Christopher nodded. "What we have discovered will be shared only with Lady Angela herself. I can tell you for certain that if you let us on our way tomorrow, Angela can contain it, and the goblins will retreat back into their holes."

Judge Craven shook his head. "Oh, I think not. We're set for a siege from an army of goblins. We can hold them off well enough, but not a dark magician able to control a force that size. And certainly not the ravages of dragons. It's a three-day ride to Angela's Haven, and if the only Enchanter here leaves, we don't stand a chance."

Christopher began to protest, but Hikaru interrupted. "I'm am Enchanter, Judge. If you will let my friend leave, I will protect Greystone. Governor Deas has never killed a dragon. I've killed hundreds."

Judge Craven's eyes widened. "Impressive, Chief Minister. But two Enchanters will be better than one. Besides, after a few days of empty highways, the Havens will send airships full of troops and see that we need aid. Imperial troops from Martinvale will be here by then, and the goblins will be routed. If they don't flee at the sight of you killing dragons, of course."

"I can get us there in two days." Manny's interjection surprised everyone in the room. "I've studied all the old maps of the ruins of Trumaria. We can cut across to Perry Ford and take horses to the Haven."

Judge Craven laughed. "You're smart, my boy. My own son is only attending the National Academy because of your patient tutelage. But old maps of that Skyborne city can hardly account for the thousand years of rot and monster infestation. Step foot within miles, and you'll find yourself full of goblin arrows – if you're lucky."

Manny's father scratched his black beard. "It might work, sir. A small, well-armed force guided by an Enchanter as powerful as a Haven Governor could survive the journey. And there's something else I've just learned." He stared at Manny.

Manny took a deep breath. "I have the gift of miracles, Judge. That's why the Enchanter is here, to see if I'm fit for study."

Christopher nodded. "Yes, he's a magician, but, well… Even a squadron of Enchanters would hesitate to go through those accursed ruins. Professors routinely watch over them from the sky, but it would be foolish to enter without their maps!"

Judge Craven slouched back and thought for a moment. "This battle will make or break the Republic. We can save the nation in the next election if we hold the line. Better so if the son of Greystone's Sheriff, an initiate Enchanter, saves us from the siege. It benefits the Havens, too. Chief Minister, you're in agreement, aren't you?"

Hikaru's nod surprised Christopher. "Your contentions are wise, Judge. Of course, it is not I who will make this journey, so I am not as anxious as my old friend. The political gains from victory are as enormous as the cost of losing. The more you bet now, the larger that chasm grows."

Manny's father smiled. "How many people will join you? Manny, Christopher, I can spare a dozen men. Constable Sana should conclude the journey with you, it's only fair for her promotion schedule."

A smile was met with Sana's frown. "With all due respect, Sheriff, I'm tired of babysitting. I'll stay here and fight with everyone else."

Manny's father was confused. "Babysitting?"

Christopher nodded awkwardly. "A young lady found a talisman. She and two of her friends attract unwanted attention because of it. You'll need to send them away."

Manny's father shook his head. "You can send the one who found a talisman, because we have no choice. Three youths will slow a unit down immeasurably."

Christopher shook his head. "The talisman's call will sound for those close to her, and she has a special bond with these two friends. Nothing peculiar, they were just practically raised together from the cradle. If they stay here, they'll aggravate the dragons."

Judge Craven chuckled. "I'm more worried about them aggravating their guards. No, Governor, it will be just the one, as Juan says. Now go spend dinner in their company; it'll be your last moment of peace before this ends."

Christopher huffed. "You're risking your City when caution is demanded. But I see there's no changing your mind. I'll do my best to prepare them." He turned and stomped out of the room.

Manny embraced his father. "I want to say goodbye to Benjamin before I go. Assuming he's at the Hirose, Judge?"

Judge Craven smiled. "We all best be saying our goodbyes. I'll want my son home tonight, just like you'll want yours, right Juan?"

Manny's father nodded. "Stay out as late as you need. I will be standing side by side with my best friend during this battle. You may not see yours again."

Hope screamed. Less out of fear and more out of surprise. A dream of being consumed by dragonfire was interrupted by her complete immersion in a tub of ice water.

"Again!" An old woman's voice cried, and a figure Hope could barely make out who doused her beneath the water once more. She growled as bubbles gurgled and water filled her nose. Thankfully, she was immediately pulled from the water and squinted at Lauren and Varsha's blurry frames.

"Wha – Wha – What – What in the name of the world was that for?" She widened her eyes and groaned even though her vision remained blurry. Any attempt to appear angry was killed by the din of her teeth chattering in the cold.

"Oh, thank God, you're awake!" Laurent reached down and hugged her tightly, shivering with her.

Hope wrapped her arms around her chest and groaned once more. "Couldn't have put me in one of the hot springs? What kind of cruel joke is this?"

The woman's voice returned, and Hope looked up with clearer vision to see a nurse. "Get her a robe. Teacup, too. This one's awake. Never fails."

Hope allowed Lauren and Varsha to help her up and out of the tub, and she hurriedly wrapped herself in a robe provided by another nurse. Within a moment, she was sitting on a bench and guzzling warm tea. After a moment to relax, she began gazing around the infirmary, realizing that the decorations were far more ornate and foreign than Dead Falls Inn.

"Does she need anything else?" Hope was surprised to see Yukio in the room.

The nurse shrugged. "She needs a good meal and a proper night's sleep. Make sure she gets two portions tonight."

Yukio smiled. "She'll have no problem here, believe me. Shall I pay you outside? They'll want a moment alone." She and the nurse vanished from the infirmary.

Hope finally finished her tea. "We're in Greystone, aren't we?"

Varsha nodded, took Hope's teacup away, and walked across the infirmary for a refill. "You gave us all a scare! Didn't realize you were that good with a knife. Have you been watching the constables practice?"

Hope shook her head before thinking back to the hot springs, slowly overcome with horror as her mind recalled every goblin she slew. "Strike me! What about Sana? Is she alright?"

Lauren nodded. "She got some bad cuts, but she's on the mend. Hikaru worked his magic. He's not quite a healer, but with his enchantments, he said Sana will be better by tomorrow morning."

Hope slouched back. "And that... that stricken old wizard. Where is he? He didn't tell me what this thing was."

Varsha returned and passed Hope the teacup. "The talisman? Don't tell me it's the Dagger of the Locust." She chuckled.

Hope took another sip and recalled the nightmares that had filled her head. "It can't be. Can it? Whatever I found is monstrous. I remember what it felt like when I... bonded with it."

Lauren grimaced. "Bonded?"

Hope took a deep breath. "Christopher warned me that I mustn't kill with it. But when they attacked, I felt it call out and promise to protect me. And by the powers, did it! I have no idea how to fight, but this thing called out to the goblins. Goaded them into attacking, one by one, knowing exactly how they'd strike, so they met their end on that blade."

Varsha tried to maintain a more cheerful mood. "Wish the cougars around Braddock would do that for me! Maybe we ought to bring it back home and take you hunting."

Hope shook her head. "I don't think we can go home. On my first night with that cursed thing, I dreamed monsters burned Braddock down. And while I slept after the attack yesterday, I had the same dream, only worse. It came after us, wherever we went."

Lauren put her hand on Hope's knee. "You just need a good meal to keep your mind off it."

Hope nodded. "I need to stretch my legs. I feel like I've been asleep for a week!"

Lauren laughed. "We won't have to wait much longer. Yukio can take us to our rooms to change, and we can go to the dining hall!"

Varsha smirked. "It'll be a great opportunity to stretch your legs. I peeked in there earlier, a lot of rich young men getting in their last meal before dying in battle. Bet most of them want their last dance, too."

Lauren was mortified. "How macabre!"

Hope looked up at Varsha and found herself smirking back. "Maybe we can make a game of it. Most dances in a night wins."

Varsha was impressed. "Maybe that talisman isn't so bad for you after all. See, Lauren? She isn't blushing like she does when I normally mention boys."

Lauren scowled. "Just leave me out of it."

Hope was far more energized than expected after a day and night of unwelcome dreams. She traveled to their room and was excited to put on a new dress with enthusiasm, marveling at the ornate Naran gowns that had been prepared for them. Hers was bright green and tied together with a striking belt, red like her hair.

Lauren winced as she brushed the last kink out of her hair. "You going to brush? Your hair got awfully frizzy."

Hope stood before a full-body mirror with her arms cocked at her hips, smiling at her natural curls. "No. It's perfect the way it is."

Lauren appeared worried. "You're not going to fetch many boys looking like that."

Hope shrugged. "I'll catch the boys ready for a spirited dance with a ginger."

Varsha smiled in approval. "Your hair does look a little frizzy, but neither of us has seen you this confident! Looking fierce, looking fierce, lovely!" Her words did not sway Lauren, who was silent on their way to the grand ballroom.

The ballroom was several times larger than the tavern hall in Braddock and infinitely finer in appearance. Murals covered the ceiling and the wall detailing famous scenes from a foreign history; Yukio pointed out that scenes were drawn from the annals of Nara. Near the far end of the hall, an elfin orchestra played songs that they had perfected over centuries of practice, setting the pace for a party of revelers that had transitioned from dinner to dancing.

An exquisite array of Naran delicacies lined the wall near the entrance, served by attendants at the pleasure of diners who had merely to offer a plate. Hope hastily accepted a small bowl of broth and noodles on her platter but hesitated at the sight of a strange concoction.

"You've not had rice like this," Yukio promised, noticing Hope's hesitation and directing a server to place something unrecognizable on Hope's plate. "It's wrapped in seaweed and paired with fish and other vegetables. You won't be disappointed." Hope shrugged and accepted the food, moving on down the line with her companions before walking to the tables.

Varsha chuckled as they sat down. "These people certainly are festive for the eve of battle. Of course, if I was wealthy and facing certain death, I'd drink myself to sleep!"

Hope dropped her spoon on the table. "What battle? Nobody mentioned a battle!"

Lauren rubbed her forehead in exhaustion. "Oh, strike me! I must be more tired than I realized. Um, Yukio, can you tell her?"

Yukio shook her head. "I can speak more once we're back in our rooms. We all know why Christopher is taking the three of you on the road, and it seems we're not the only ones. I don't know the depth of the danger, but this city is on the brink of a goblin siege. I'm thankful that the Hotel's courtyard has its own strong gates, because the city is tearing itself apart."

Hope began to panic. "Well, we can't stay here! Why aren't we on the road? I feel fine enough to travel now!"

Yukio shook her head. "The nurse said you will need to get your rest. Now that I think about it, you'll probably need a few bowls of that ramen. Christopher is visiting the Sheriff; he will inform us when we can depart."

Hope stared down at her bowl of soup, lazily stirring her spoon. "This is all my fault. I should never have-"

"Quiet!" Varsha shook her head. "We don't know who may be listening. Stop feeling sorry for yourself, eat up, and dance with a boy until he can't stand! We can worry about getting on the road tomorrow."

Yukio smiled. "Yes, try the sashimi!" She picked up her own seaweed-wrapped rice and chewed with a look of complete satisfaction. Hope slowly picked up one of the rice wraps, eyes popping in favor as she rapidly swallowed it down and funneled the remaining pieces into her mouth.

After eating her fill, Hope leaned back and jubilantly patted her stomach. "Strike me... Forget Angela's Haven, I want to board the first ship to Nara!"

"Shh!" Lauren remained anxious.

Varsha pointed toward Hope's soup bowl. "Try the ramen. I'm definitely going for seconds!"
Hope used a thin pair of filed sticks to dig into her noodles, awkwardly wrapping them around before discovering the proper technique to lift a few into her mouth.

Hope shrugged after a few pleasant but challenging mouthfuls. "Well, if they weren't so difficult to eat, they'd be alright."

Varsha laughed. "Takes some getting used to, but I'm going to try and have mom's servants make this. The Narans know how to eat!"

Lauren seemed to relax a little bit more. "It's quite an experience, getting to know a culture through its cuisine. I hear the cooking students at the National Academy provide a different type of food for the school each week!"

Varsha laughed. "That might make an education worthwhile." Looking up, she espied a young man with strong arms and a chiseled jaw. "You two keep eating; I'm going to sample some of the local boys."

Hope winked. "Save some for us! I'm going to dance with at least three tonight."

Varsha patted Hope's shoulder. "I never thought you'd have the nerve for a game like this. May the best woman win!" She excused herself and began wading through the tables, straight back and seductive smile projected toward the young men dining with their parents.

Lauren's anxiety returned, but she struggled to articulate her worry. "But... what about Manny?"

"Who?" Hope laughed when Lauren looked shocked at the suggestion she had lost her memory. "I jest, you know that.

He's nice and all. But we only just met! And he's not here. Which means someone else gets the chance to sweep me off my feet."

Lauren huffed. "What's gotten into you?"

Hope shook her head. "Whatever do you mean?"

Lauren pursed her lips. "Don't blame it on... You know what. That thing. You disrupted the whole tavern on your birthday, and we all went to jail because of it! And I didn't see... well, whatever happened at Dead Falls, but what you described is just... Well, it's not you. And here you are, ogling boys like fruit at the market with Varsha!"

Hope smirked. "Ooh, that's exactly what I'm doing! Except I'm going to make them haggle for me!"

Lauren frowned and shook her head. "This isn't like you! When did you ever dance in Braddock? You're usually in the corner reading with me. Varsha's supposed to be the wild one!"

Hope turned and stared Lauren directly in the eyes. "My destiny has been handed to me for as long as I can remember. But nobody knows the future, and I won't let myself be groomed for an uncontrollable destiny. In fact, I think I'm going make my move right now." She got up from the table and marched toward a well-dressed boy who had been watching them, ignoring Lauren's pleas for her to return to a banal conversation. The boy seemed intrigued by Hope's approach, responding to her seductive smile with a look of surprised exhilaration.

She sat next to him at his otherwise empty table, guessing by the look of a second platter of uneaten food that he was waiting for someone. "I see I caught your eye. Call me Hope."

The youth raised an eyebrow. "You know, a thousand young women swoon at me every day, but none have ever had the courage to ask for my attention. A dance you shall have!"

Hope followed him onto the floor and observed the other dancers, quickly stepping as they did. After a few awkward moments, she eased into the rhythm and allowed her partner to lead her on the floor.

Her partner affectionately squeezed her shoulder. "Are you from Martinvale? You've got the hair of an Airgiallan, even if you don't talk like one."

Hope shook her head. "Good guess, but I'm from the hill country. Never stepped foot in the Empire."

Her partner smiled. "Well, you wouldn't be the first to pursue the freedom the Republic offers. Greystone is full of expatriates seeking refuge from the pettiness of monarchy and mercantilism. Any man can be what he wants in the Republic, and nowhere is that truer than Greystone!"

Hope was unimpressed with the turn to politics. "You must love your city. Is that because it's treason not to?"

Her partner frowned. "We don't blindly follow Yorkton's lead here. My father allows anyone to speak out as they please, against himself or even the Chancellor!"

"Your father?"

The youth chuckled. "Strike me, I'm forgetting my manners. Benjamin Craven, son of Judge Gunther Craven."

Hope was taken aback. "I'm dancing with Greystone royalty! The second I've met this week."

Benjamin cocked his head. "If Ricky was too forward, I'm happy to knock him down a peg. He means well, but he can be a little forceful."

Hope looked up for a minute. "Um, no, never met a Ricky. The one I met is the son of the Sheriff. Quite that talker.

Benjamin stopped dancing. "Manny? No, must be an imposter. He's not even said hello to a girl who wasn't his cousin. Painfully awkward, that one. You must be something special to draw his attention."

Hope laughed. "I'm sort of… Opening up for the first time. It may be drawing him out."

Benjamin winked. "Well, Manny deserves to have a beautiful girl by his side. Most of the girls in town find him a bit too impish, but you won't find a purer heart around."

Hope blushed. "Awe, but I liked his delicate features. More for me, I suppose."

Benjamin smiled and nodded his head forward. "You can tell him that now."

Hope tried to put her head down and placed a hand on the side of her face. "Oh strike me, you don't think he sees, do you?"

Benjamin shrugged. "Doesn't matter, I'm his best friend. He's coming over here anyway."

Hope looked up and turned toward an approaching memory, trying her best to placate his look of horror with a broad but obviously fake smile.

Manny realized he was looking and tried to smile awkwardly. "Hope, nice to see you awake."

Benjamin shook his head. "You'll need to flirt better than that, old chum. Makes it sound like you've been watching her sleep."

Manny cringed. "She was ill!"

Benjamin rolled his eyes. "Oh, be discrete! She's entitled to her decency."

Manny sighed deeply. "Hope, I just, uh... Well, Christopher will be in shortly. He's in the lobby with Hikaru. You might want to go to your room and-"

"Hope!" The Enchanter shouted above the music, causing a nearby Sana to cover her ears in annoyance. "Over here, at once." His glare reverberated across the ballroom and shortly led to the appearance of Lauren, Varsha, and Yukio. "Young lady, you should have known better than to let these three out of your rooms! Hikaru will be most displeased."

Yukio hung her head. "My apologies, Governor. A nurse recommended that Hope eat to recover her strength."

Christopher remained angry. "She could have eaten in her room! Should have! Strike me, you're all going to get us killed!"

Benjamin put up his hand. "Pardon me, Enchanter, they were just enjoying the splendor of their county seat. My father wishes Greystone to be home to all."

Christopher was mystified at first, but he soon relaxed. "Pardon me, young Mr. Craven. Your hospitality is appreciated, but we must depart. Hope, is it safe?"

Hope looked down at her belt and realized the Dagger was gone. "Oh, it should be in our hotel room."

Christopher raised an eyebrow. "Should be, or is?"

Yukio gasped. "No, it isn't." Christopher glared, and she began to whisper. "Garments were taken to a washroom. It... it will be with her dress."

Christopher slammed his staff on the ground. "Lauren, Varsha, to your rooms this instant! Manny, Hope, with me. We're going to grab... it, and you will stay in your rooms until morning. Understood?" He huffed and headed out of the ballroom, his wards following silently behind.

"Hikaru!" Christopher paid no attention to etiquette as he barged into a private room where the diplomat was enjoying an evening drink with the innkeeper, a distant cousin. "I must go to the Hotel's washer at once. *It* has been misplaced."

"Pardon me, you don't mean Hope's, um..." Hikaru struggled to find a replacement word for the Dagger.

Sana interjected awkwardly. "Knitting needle."

Hope raised an eyebrow. "There's more than one needle in knitting."

Sana cringed. "Pair of knitting needles. That pair, it's gone."

Hikaru frowned. "Ah, yes, the knitting needles." Hikaru sighed, turning to his cousin to explain the situation in their native Naran language. Annoyed by the interruption, the innkeeper sighed and wrote instructions on a loose piece of paper.

Offering an unintelligible valediction, Hikaru bowed to the innkeeper and motioned Christopher's party out the door. "It's at a washroom nearby. I'll lead us there." He wanted a good night's sleep before battle; now he was stuck ferrying an

Enchanter, a constable, the son of the Sheriff, and a woman possibly possessed by a demon through a terrified city.

Christopher spoke after a few moments, silently navigating toward the hotel exit. "The incompetence is inexcusable, I know." Hope immediately lowered her head in shame, and Sana glared at him in objection to the punishment.

Hikaru found room to appear sympathetic, worried about upsetting the bearer of a Deathlord's talisman after the attack on Dead Falls. "Nobody is ever trained to handle a demon's talisman. I'm glad we didn't reach Angela's Haven before realizing the sewing needles were lost." Hikaru's rebuke of Christopher's worry seemed to lighten Hope's mood, a silent sigh of relief sounding through her breath.

Christopher seemed eager to change the subject. "I hope it isn't far from here."

Hikaru looked at the instructions on the note and shrugged. "We must hurry down a few side streets, but it will allow us to avoid the market, so we should be there in minutes." His estimation soon proved grossly optimistic, as the process of negotiating an exit from the Hotel proved difficult. Loud crowds beyond the gates of the inn's courtyard barely allowed Hikaru to think, even with his species' innate ability to drown out noise. As the guards opened the gate with a foot-wide gap, Sana's hands maintained a white-knuckled grasp on the hilt of her sword, and Hope marveled at the ponds and gardens of the courtyard one last time.

Hikaru finally found the right moment to face the throng. "Now!" He jumped through the gate while the guards waved Christopher and the others forward.

He turned and saw Christopher trying to manage a nervous Hope. "Take my hand!" The Enchanter reached back to grab Hope and pull her through the excited crowd. Any moment, Hikaru believed, the people would tear through every locked door in the city, scavenging for food and weapons, ravaging Greystone into oblivion before the approaching dragons appeared on the horizon.

Hikaru stopped once they reached the other side of the street, glancing down at the napkin before motioning them to take a left turn and follow along the side of the road. The street remained thick with a mass of hectic residents, parting the roads only for heavily guarded wagons and carriages ferrying soldiers and nobles through the city. He was thankful that he had worn a dark cloak that night. The rest of the party was dressed gaudily, and he prayed they would not draw undue attention. That they remained unmolested, Hikaru attributed to the scowl and constable uniform Sana wore.

"Look out!" Hikaru cried suddenly as they approached a new byway. His outstretched arm knocked Christopher back, and he gazed in horror upon the spectacle of a carriage crashing into a wagon. Soldiers on both vehicles were thrown away as horses wailed in terror, creating chaos that invited pedestrians to swarm the accident and pillage for unguarded food and weapons.

"Strike me!" Hikaru grumbled. "We'll have to go through the market. Prepare to fight for your lives in there."

Christopher nodded, tightening the grip on his staff as he led Hope and Sana in Hikaru's path toward the market. Hikaru's worst fears of looting were realized as they came upon a packed alleyway filled with people desperately tearing through long-empty food stands and boxes, hoping to find supplies even in unrelated packages from the Ikeda Shoe Company.

A vagrant cream or up on Sana. "Hey! How much for the sword?"

Sana growled. "Slough off!"

The vagrant continued to follow. "You're not a real constable, so you must have got it somewhere… if you could buy that one, you can buy another." He reached an intrusive hand toward Sana's arm, but she immediately shoved him into a crowd of looters.

Angry, the man jumped up and shouted. "She's got food!"

"Food?" A dozen looters from all walks of life immediately rushed in Sana's direction, and she whipped out her cutlass to slash at them in self-defense.

"Christopher, time to work your magic!" Sana drew blood from an attacker but ducked as one swung a metal bar at her.

"You will leave us at once!" Christopher shouted, his voice growing in volume as his height increased. The looters ran from the sight, terrified by the Enchanter's display of power and hoping to avoid being his victims.

"That's not fair!" The vagrant who had accosted Sana stared dejectedly. "You've got a magician, I don't even have a knife!"

Sana growled. "You'll have even less if you say another word!"

"You lot live for yourselves!" The vagrant finally ran away.

Hikaru rushed through the bazaar as the looters cleared a path for the party. "Come, we surely haven't much time!" He led his companions through another street into a small town square, eerily unoccupied except for a scurrying pair of rats. "That... that should be it." He pointed at a darkened storefront, lights off and doors wide open. "We may be too late."

Hope was oddly cheerful. "No, I'm sure it's there."

Christopher turned to look at his ward, surprised at the suggestion that she could sense the Dagger's presence. "What do you mean?"

Hope shrugged. "I felt like I was missing something when I awoke earlier. But now I feel like I'm... complete."

Hikaru and Christopher exchanged understanding glances, expecting the worst. "Christopher, say when. Sana, Manny, guard the door." The constable nodded silently, withdrawing her bloodied sword from its sheath. Manny appeared disappointed, but he obediently waited outside.

Christopher had to clamp his hand down on Hope's mouth unexpectedly as they entered the washer, bloodied bodies strewn between steaming vats of water. He pulled his hand away suddenly at the sensation of something wet meeting his hand, and he turned to see tears streaming down Hope's face.

The young woman gasped. "It's all because of me. They're dead because of me!"

Sana knelt down in front of Hope, placing a hand on her arm in comfort as she said, "Hope, you can't think about that right now. Our actions have consequences, but if we focus on them, we can't fix them. If you can... sense that the Dagger is near, you need to grab it and let us depart."

Hikaru was thankful that Sana took on the task of comforting the distraught girl, and he prayed for Hope's head to clear as she closed her eyes to sense the Dagger's pull. He and Christopher were both intrigued by Hope's tactic, realizing that they were learning more about the talisman than had been discerned by all past scholars.

"It's... over there?" Hope warily pointed behind a vat of clothes, hesitating before nodding confidently. "Yes, it's there, I'm sure of it." Christopher responded to a questioning expression from Hikaru by shrugging, and he remained by the door as Hope led the elf in the right direction.

"It's here!" Hope cried in relief the moment she went around a large vat, only to jump back in horror and flee past Hikaru. He immediately brandished his sword, shocked to lock blades with a feral young woman whose eyes had turned completely black. As he fought back against her wild attacks, he surmised that she had gotten ahold of the Dagger when it arrived, proceeding to kill.

"You deserve peace." Hikaru conjured massive boils on her eyelids, and as she leaped at him blindly, she impaled her neck on his sword, falling backward with a gurgling thud. He turned and saw a terrified Hope tightly clinging to a fearful Christopher.

"I don't want it. I... I can't do this." Hope shook her head ferociously.

Hikaru began to clean his blade. "The moment you pick a sword, it is with the intent to kill. One must always remember. Right now, that blade is on the floor, free for the taking. The last person who picked it up killed everyone in the room. You are the only one who can pick it up, and you must, because only you can put it back in its sheath where it won't take another life." He smiled warmly, sheathing his sword and reaching forth a hand. Hope nervously walked forward and picked up the Dagger, nervously wiping the blade on the dead woman's dress.

"Wizard! A little help out here!" They nervously looked toward the doorway Sana was yelling from, wary as militiamen with torches approached. The trio walked through the door, and Hikaru nervously gripped the hilt of his sword.

A soldier smirked. "It's after curfew. Be a shame if any of you were to break it."

Manny nervously stared him in the eye. "I'm Sheriff Alonso's son. Have a problem with me, take it up to him."

The soldier ignored him and turned to a comrade. "What color dress did Skurlag say she wore? Green? We're mighty lucky."

Hikaru unsheathed his sword once again. "Don't presume you're getting out of here alive. That name is your death warrant."

The soldier wordlessly threw his head back and let out a crazed laugh, eerily emulated by his four compatriots. Swords drawn, they charged forward, swinging their swords wildly. Hikaru, Sana, and Christopher immediately formed a shield around Hope and Manny. Hikaru dispatched two, and Sana dispatched one, while Christopher found himself a poorer staff-wielder than his opponents were swordsmen.

One pushed past the Enchanter and lunged at Manny, who warded him off by conjuring flame around his cutlass blade. Christopher finally bested his attacker, and the marauder facing Manny tries to slash at a blind spot. Manny ferociously lashed out, white-hot fire snaking from his sword and melting the attacker's blade.

Sensing no escape, the attacker pulled a knife from his belt and stabbed himself in the gut, falling to the ground. "For... Skurlag..." The pronouncement caused everyone to shudder.

Hikaru cleaned his blade once more. "Take her back to the Hirose this instant! Manny and I will warn his father. If the Locust can reach this far into Greystone already, we have far more to worry about than dragons.

Chapter 6: Unwelcome Valedictions

The city could be burning. Was it? Was every human soul a lit match, lighting other matches and setting fire to thatched roofs and oaken door frames? Her spirit soaring high above Greystone, Hope could see a trail of flames leaping about the city amidst screams and violent outbursts. None of this could continue, the fire must be put out at the source! She willed herself to follow the trail of flames, passing hovels near the wall to unfamiliar streets before she espied the Courthouse, then the washroom and market, and finally, the courtyard of Hirose Hotel.

Perspective switched suddenly as her eyes became glued to the window of the bedroom where she rested, curtains parting of their own accord as she froze in place to gaze upon the snarling face of a dragon. The beast smirked at her, smoke pouring from its nostrils as she lay bound to her bed, unable to cry out to Lauren or Varsha. The dragon's fire consumed their hotel instantly, and she found herself carried aloft once again, staring in horror at the charred remains of her friends. In the courtyard below, Christopher's blackened staff lay beside his torn sash, clutched in Sana's skeletal hand.

Greystone itself was in ruins, the flaming souls having torn the city asunder with greater haste than any goblin army. The creatures infested the city before her eyes, taking what they would and cutting through the living souls who remained to cry out in terror. Hope looked down and realized the dragon was carrying her, triumphantly circling the city as its rider held the Dagger high in the air. As desperately as Hope tried to throw the weapon away, it would not leave her grasp, almost seeming to laugh at her frustration.

Finally, the dragon landed on the field before Greystone, the legions of goblins immediately kneeling as Hope dismounted. The same paralysis that had kept her from warning her friends of a dragon attack once again cemented her feet to the ground, and the Dagger itself seemed to float into the air, carrying her arm with it.

"We are one again!" A new voice called, seeming to emanate from the Dagger. Its bold pronouncement was delivered in unison with Hope, and she was terrified by the eerie voice of ten thousand goblins crying in response. "You are one again!"

Each goblin's head slowly faded from its body, cascading into a river of tears wept by the mothers of Braddock and Yorkton. Images of cities Hope had only seen in books came to life in their full glory for one moment before dragons circled and goblins swarmed, city dwellers joining the invaders' ranks or losing their heads. The darkness spread over Manifest, crossing the oceans to Nova and Shaolin with little resistance before consuming the remaining world, after which a satisfied Hope smiled at the Dagger and looked to the stars.

The voice spoke again. "We will be one. We will be one."

Hope repeated the voice, fearing the consequences of saying no. "We will be one. We will be one, we will be one!" She cringed as the Dagger's hand guards tightened around her fist and then consumed her like a cocoon, but in a final act, she was defiant. "I will not be one!"

"Hope! What are you going on about?"

Eyes wide open, Hope reflexively moved her hand and shook with fear, recalling the horrors she had endured in her dream. Fear coursed strongly through her veins, a current of darkness washing through a forest after a dreadful storm. Nervously moving her eyes back and forth, Hope adjusted to the lack of light before turning her head at Lauren in the bed beside hers and sighing.

"Nothing. Go back to sleep."

"Sleep? At a time like this?" Varsha sounded like she was sitting up in her bed. "I'm going to see my first battle tomorrow! I mean, shame we won't be staying for it, but still, I'd like to see the goblins approaching before we leave!"

Lauren growled. "You won't live to see it if you don't go back to sleep."

Hope said nothing, wishing that her friends would slumber before Christopher arrived to secretly whisk her away. Memories of the previous night flooded back as she saw the delirious ferocity of the washerwoman who had accidentally found the Dagger in her clothes. That same power coursed through her veins now, and Hope wondered if she looked that way when she fought goblins at Dead Falls. She also wondered why she had been able to quiet the Dagger's hold when the other woman had not. Perhaps it was because the Dagger had bonded with her already, or maybe something much darker already hid within her soul that synced perfectly with the talisman by her side.

Christopher's inconvenient knock at the door disturbed Lauren first. "That better be a free breakfast." Her blanket rumpled loudly as she covered her head.

"Breakfast!" Varsha was up first, jaunting toward the door and letting light inside their room to reveal the Enchanter. "You whetted my appetite for this?"

Christopher was puzzled. "What in the name of the world? You ought to be asleep, young lady! Oh, strike me…"

Hope quietly got out of bed, already wearing her clothes for the day. "I'm leaving now." She said nothing more as she reached down to grab her bag for the road.

Varsha gasped. "You weren't going to leave us here, were you? What's gotten into you?"

Lauren bolted upright. "Hope? What's happening?"

Hope sighed deeply. "I wish you'd been awake when I returned last night. Only I'm allowed to go. The Judge seems to think you two will make a fine ransom to ensure that the Haven comes to rescue Greystone."

Varsha was livid. "That ape! We should go to the courthouse to beat his sense back into his head!"

Hope shook her head. "No, it's for the best. You two, something happened last night…" She paused and stared wistfully at Christopher, who shrugged at her. "A washerwoman found the Dagger and... she went mad. Absolutely lost her virtue. She killed everyone else at the wash. Hikaru had to use magic to defeat her. I know what's inside this thing now, and I don't want it to hurt anyone else. The sooner I can take it to Angela's Haven, the sooner I can be rid of it."

Varsha huffed. "Well, I don't have to like it. Besides, I'd rather be with the woman who can kill a hundred goblins alone. I mean, I'll be fine if they make it in here. Lauren, though-"

"That's not funny!" Lauren shivered. "We won't survive four days of being attacked by dragons. Going to Angela's Haven was our only guarantee of survival! Christopher, how could you risk that?"

Christopher hung his head. "It gives me no pleasure. Your parents will give me a lashing for it, so don't waste your anger on me. But the Judge was quite firm in his orders that you two are to stay. Now, both of you get a good rest while you can. Sleep all day if you like. Hikaru will see to your care. If the worst should happen and the city should fall, he knows to rescue both of you. There is nobody I trust more with your protection."

Varsha rolled her eyes. "Well, just let me do one thing." She stomped toward Hope, stared deep into her eyes, and embraced her tightly. It was a rare display of affection that made Hope finally relax. Her anxiety was further quelled when Lauren got up from her bed and hugged her tightly. She could feel tears from both her friends, and in another time, she would also be sobbing. But the Dagger had robbed her of something, leaving a wall between her and the emotions that welled within her soul.

Christopher cleared his throat. "Alright, it's time to go. We must depart before sunlight to avoid being seen."

Hope withdrew from her friends and patted them both on the shoulder. "I love you both dearly. Pray for me, and I'll pray for you. We have a plan to get to the Haven in two days, not four. We'll outrace the dragons, don't worry."

Varsha's eyes widened. "You're going through Trumaria! Awe, now I'm going to kill that Judge!"

Hope laughed as Varsha winked after her pronouncement, only partially jesting. "Tell you what, if I survive, I'll take you through next time."

Her journey from the room to the fields east of Greystone was a blur. Christopher led her downstairs to meet Manny, Sana, and Hikaru, where they walked through the unlit hotel courtyard and joined a party of a dozen soldiers outside. Hope awkwardly mounted her own steed and found herself quite awkwardly navigating the creature, cursing her lifelong disinterest in riding. She was shocked by how calm the city had become, the main streets empty and darkened under a brilliantly starry sky. Perhaps the city had gone to sleep once she had, the Dagger's energy failing to radiate once she drifted into the world of dreams. Once she was gone, the city would be at peace enough with itself to stand a chance against the goblin onslaught.

Hope found herself utterly unprepared as the other riders began to gallop once they left the city gates. As Christopher called for her to keep up, she was embarrassed to find that she trailed behind the other riders. She never needed to take a horse on more than a slow trot, and the rush from barely holding onto the reins as her horse rushed forward made her lose focus. A mile from the gates, Hope finally lost the strength to command the animal and began to slow. Sana was the first to notice, shouting at Christopher that she would take care of Hope.

"I'm sorry." Hope called to Sana as she nudged her horse toward the approaching constable. "I've never galloped before! It's a little scary."

Sana looked down and shook her head. "No wonder you're having trouble! Those stirrups are much too long for you. Christopher, we're stopping!" The constable dismounted and moved toward Hope's saddle, adjusting the straps so that Hope's feet were more firmly planted in the stirrups.

She nodded as Christopher trotted over. "Better?"

"What in the name of the world are you doing?" Christopher shook his head. "We don't have time to make stops like this!"

Sana's eyes burned. "Give her a minute, wizard! She's never had to gallop on a horse before, much less flee dragons. She's unpracticed, and she needs to at least be able to plant her feet firmly if she's going to get this beast moving forward."

Christopher snickered. "You could've at least waited until we were in the woods!"

Sana let out a sarcastic laugh. "Ha! We've got ten miles to go through these fields before we reach the forest! We take care of problems when they happen, not when they get worse."

Christopher responded with a cold stare, but even he was taken aback by the glare he met in Sana's eyes. Retreating from his battle, the Enchanter turned his horse around and began galloping back toward the forest without a word.

Hope sighed. "Thank you, Sana. I didn't realize how loose my stirrups were."

Sana nodded. "Everyone here has quite a bit to learn. For all they know of magic, wizards are blind to the needs of people around them."

Hope shrugged in concurrence. "I'm just glad you're here to stick up for me."

Sana's eyes shifted uncomfortably, and she turned to mount her horse. "I'm just here to stick up for the laws of the Republic. And I'm not keen to lose someone again."

Hope trotted her horse forward and tried to gain speed alongside Sana. "Who did you lose?"

Sana shook her head. "It ain't storytime. Now gallop, or everything's lost." The constable kicked her horse forward, leaving Hope in the dust.

As she caught up to the party, she saw one horse slow to the back and smiled at seeing Manny's face. "Hey, are you feeling alright?"

Hope struggled to speak over the sound of the horses. "Much better now! Who knew stirrups would be so important?"

Manny shook his head. "I meant with your friends and all. Having to leave them behind must be hard."

Hope nodded but straightened quickly as she felt wobbly. "I can't afford to think about it. My head is so full of unwelcome thoughts that I can't think straight. I just have to try to be happy..." She shivered as her head drowned in bitter memories of monsters and men consumed by violence.

"Hope?" Manny's voice was louder than usual.

Hope realized she had been so lost in thought that she did not hear him. "What?"

Manny smiled weakly. "I was asking if it had anything to do with... you know."

"With... sorry." Hope took a deep breath. "I can barely hear over the sound of these horses!" She chuckled awkwardly, pulling away a hand from the reins to gently slap the horse in jest, only to nearly fall from her saddle as she lost balance.

Manny slowed his horse as Hope brought her steed down to a trot. "Easy there! Takes a while to learn how to ride one of these properly. When my friend Benjamin and I learned, we would tease each other for falling off! Eventually, you fear falling off more than riding. Then you learn to stay on top."

Hope smiled genuinely for the first time that morning. "Well, with someone like you teaching me, maybe we can avoid that part."

Manny winked. "Nothing to it. Keep your feet planted in your stirrups, and don't let go of the reins!"

Hope winked back. "It'll be easier if you don't distract me."

Manny cringed. "I would never! I..." He began to smirk back as he realized Hope was joking. "I'm sure the ghosts will do that for me!"

Hope shook and fought to quickly regain her balance. "Ghosts? You mean in Trumaria?"

Manny laughed. "They say the city is full of evil spirits from the days of the Skyborne. Maps of the ocean show serpeants, and maps of the mountains show dragons. All of the maps around Trumaria say, 'Here be ghosts!'"

Hope remained anxious. "Will one Enchanter be enough?"

Manny somehow remained jocular. "The City was torn to shreds during the Uprising a thousand years ago. Any ghost that survived probably doesn't have all of its limbs attached. It's been abandoned so long, they probably forgot how to scare people!"

His humor slightly helped allay her worries. "You better be right. For their sake. If what I have can slay goblins, imagine what it will do to demons."

Manny seemed to grow uneasy, but Hope took the opportunity to move a hand off the reins and gently squeeze the hilt of her Dagger. Somehow, she felt comforted that the weapon that conquered goblins would vanquish even the most frightful ghosts.

Hikaru had not fought in battle for over a century, tired long ago of wielding magic to take life rather than improve it. He had remained a tactician nonetheless, performing statecraft for the Havens and the court of Naran Empress Takara. Now, Hikaru had to dust off his knowledge of strategy and think back to the antiquated battlefields of Eastern Cathay. Still, before he recalled his command of half-breed legions, he needed to ensure the safety of two human girls.

It seemed like a hopeless venture - of all the thinking races the world over, he found young human women to be only slightly less intolerable than half-breeds. Of course, were the world rid of young human ladies, there would be no more humans, male or otherwise, and he immensely admired the species' tenacity. Half-breeds, on the other hand, lacked any redeeming qualities, and Hikaru was thankful that they had finally sequestered themselves in their own nation over a century ago. Their liberator could play President until the world's societies finally stamped out the plague of miscegenation, and he found himself alone in a crumbling palace.

After spending the morning praying and meditating, Hikaru descended to the dining hall of the Hirose Hotel and met with Yukio, Lauren, and Varsha. The hall was much less crowded, visiting diners and dancers having left in the night. Only a handful of lodgers remained to stir their spoons in ornate dishes.

Yukio stood up from the table and bowed, Lauren clumsily following her example. Varsha stayed put, the only person in the dining hall consuming her meal with vigor. Hikaru bowed back at Yukio and Lauren before sitting as a server arrived with his breakfast platter. The taste of home was just what he needed, and he sat momentarily, taking in the aroma of rice, miso soup, grilled fish, pickled vegetables, poached eggs, and fermented soybeans.

"That's going to go bad if you don't eat it." Varsha's chatter invited a lesson.

Hikaru slowly sipped a spoonful of miso. "Young lady, this table is more than a simple meal. These recipes come from my grandmother. Whenever I smell her cooking, I remember celebrating festivals in my childhood. And she is not alone in being honored. These dishes have filled the bellies of everyone from farmers to emperors in Nara for 1,500 years. And let us not forget that they came from the Skyborne before, traveling from the heavens to reach our lips. One does not simply eat something this old quickly."

Varsha snorted and looked at Yukio. "He always like this?"

Hikaru made a show of dropping his hand on the table near his teacup. "You have not learned to respect your elders, young lady. Do the *Feminine Virtues* mean nothing to you?"

Lauren anxiously shook her head, but Varsha smirked. "Yeah, it was the first book I ever threw down a well! Madame

Wanda never even raised any children, so I have no idea why any adult would take her words seriously."

Hikaru looked at Yukio, who nodded solemnly. "Varsha, I read the *Feminine Virtues* to prepare for our tour of the Republic. It is indeed bland. Some of its proclamations have no place in a woman's mind. But rules about respect and humility are universal, and you are disregarding all of them."

Varsha shrugged. "Respect is earned. I don't know you, Hikaru. When my mother hears he left me with you, she will box Christopher's ears. You've only got one thing going for you."

Hikaru raised an eyebrow. "Oh?"

Varsha filled her mouth with a large spoonful of rice and pickled vegetables. "You like to eat. Not just to gorge, you've invented your own special way of enjoying a meal. Not much innovation in stuffing your gut, but you, sir, have done it!"

Hikaru let his eyelids droop. "Words like yours will not invite the company of the wise, young lady. If you honor the people around you, they will honor you."

Varsha thought for a moment before smirking once more. "Just like you honored the Doryians?"

Hikaru's frown nearly broke his jaw. "Half-breeds have no honor to share. You have not been in their company, you do not know the ferocity lurking within them. Their only use is on the battlefield. And if your Republic was not so foolish as to send them to their glorified shoe factory in Shaolin, they could have been here as a bulwark against the approaching goblins. Remember the true enemy at your doorstep."

Yukio put a finger in front of her mouth before Varsha could respond. "Please, Varsha, we have a few difficult days ahead. Let us dine in peace for one final moment."

Hikaru nodded. "You would do well to listen to my pupil. The enemy will assault the gates soon enough. We cannot allow ourselves to do our work for them."

Varsha prepared to open her mouth once again, but she was discouraged by a cautious glance from Lauren. Hikaru restrained himself from rolling his eyes, annoyed that he had taken on the care of such an uncultured ward when he needed to focus on defending a city. Thankfully, Yukio maintained their silence at the table, preventing even Lauren from opening her mouth. While he believed that she would likely offer intelligent conversation, the young needed to learn to speak only when addressed by their elders.

Hikaru sat back and patted his belly once he had finished his meal. "We ought to be grateful to share such a tranquil meal on the last peaceful morning. I cannot promise I will be present over the next few days, so I must trust that you will obey the rules I have set out for you. Christopher expects you to follow my instructions, so you must respect me as you would him."

Varsha shrugged. "I just met him a few days ago. Not much going on there for me."

Hikaru remained stoic. "Then respect me more as the one who will bring you to safety if the city falls. First and foremost, you need to stay in this hotel. My family employs a hundred trained Naran warriors at each inn, and they will protect you even if the city is breached. This hotel is a citadel and will hold far longer than the rest of this town.

"Yukio shall watch over you in my absence, and I must insist you obey her commands. She will tell you when to eat, sleep, and stay in your room. I doubt I will have time to return to the hotel during the siege, so anything that must be communicated to me will go through her.

"Lastly, there is always a chance that the battle will go ill, the dragons will prove too formidable, or the goblins be more well-armed than supposed. Should the city fall, you must stay in the hotel and wait for me to come for you. Your only hope for a safe evacuation is with me. Understood?"

Lauren spoke up before Varsha could prattle. "Yes sir, Minister! Your hospitality is most gracious. We will do as you say."

Hikaru bowed his head and then turned to Varsha. "Have you chosen to be virtuous, you lady?"

Varsha's eyebrows went up and down. "Stay in the hotel, do what Yukio says, don't leave until you come for us. Don't worry, we won't be going anywhere."

Hikaru smirked back. "It's a wonder what a good meal will do for the temper. I should hope to be so clear-headed." He had no choice but to believe his wards, and he wiped his mouth on a cloth napkin before departing to the Citadel.

The state of the defenders was shameful but not unexpected for a nation that had been nominally at peace for most of its history. Constables, militia, and volunteers drilled under the watchful eye of what appeared to be Airgiallan military observers. These men would take a month to transform into effective soldiers, and their tutor had a few hours.

Hikaru found the same frenetic buzz inside the great hall of the Citadel, scouts pouring in with new information about the approaching goblin forces. Information was gamed out on a large table map where pieces were placed to represent troops from both sides. Sheriff Alonso was at the center of it all, calming the fighters in his presence.

"Minister!" The Sheriff waved Hikaru over to his side. "I want you to lead the defense of the Western gate. Are you able?"

Hikaru raised an eyebrow. "Have you no commanders of your own capable enough for command?"

Sheriff Alonso shook his head. "Nobody with your experience. My senior staff saw combat during the last Skraeling border dispute, which was open warfare. None of us know when best to fire our siege engines."

Hikaru scratched the stubble he had let loose on his bead. "And what engines do you have?"

Sheriff Alonso sighed. "Mostly repeating crossbow batteries along the walls. We have some wheeled catapults that we can deploy behind the wall, but they are still being assembled."

Hikaru furrowed his brow. "It may not be of great importance. What are your scouts seeing? I don't anticipate goblins will have anything too threatening. Maybe battering rams. Siege towers, trebuchets, ballistae – those would be far too complex for a goblin force this far from Grennan."

Sheriff Alonso nodded. "You're correct. They're felling lots of trees. Few of them have real armor, so the few that make it to the gate won't last long."

"And just how many are there?"

The Sheriff looked down at the table. "About three thousand have crawled out from the hill country. I have five hundred constables, a couple thousand militia, and the civilians training. I pray it's enough."

Hikaru stared at the map and thought about the strategy he expected. "And the dragons?"

Sheriff Alonso shivered. "One is headed east, over the forest. The other flew north, who knows why. But that's the one that I expect will attack the city."

Hikaru eyed the map once more. "I trust Manny told you about the incident last night. Have you told your men to be on the lookout for traitors?"

The Sheriff sighed. "It was a difficult decision, but yes. Everyone is fearful enough, but now my men must look over their shoulders for fear of bewitched comrades. Soldiers should be worried about looking forward, not backward. If dark magic is weaving through my ranks, it will be…"

Hikaru finished the sentence that Sheriff Alonso could not. "It'll be a bloodbath."

A nearby constable shook. "Bloodbath!"

Hikaru frowned. "For them, obviously! Sheriff, tell that one to be useless elsewhere."

Sheriff Alonso smiled. "Relax, we're all frightened. What do you foresee?"

Hikaru took a deep breath. "They want to make the people afraid. Goblins and witches have become fairy tales, like dragons. Fading into memory. Even the attacks on the hill country haven't been bad enough for the Republic to intervene until now. If they are felling trees but lack armaments, the dark magician controlling them does not expect to win a siege by strength of arms alone. They need us to be afraid and divided to ensure their victory. Dark magic will be concentrated on the siege, so I do not expect to see them turn any more of your men. Leave the defense of the Western gate to me, and don't worry about the goblins."

Sheriff Alonso looked worried. "Oh?"

Hikaru shook his head, and the Sheriff's anxiety returned. "Worry about the dragons. If the beast bound for the north returns, it will strike from above, raining fire and striking at soldiers. Prepare archers and javelin throwers to hide on your highest towers so that they can distract it from the true threat."

Sheriff Alonso squinted. "And what is the true threat to a dragon?"

Hikaru smirked. "Me."

Manny's legs had tired of riding by noon, and he was thankful when the rest order came from the party's leader, a constable named Richard Flanagan.

"Nonsense!" Christopher tried to continue riding as the constables stopped. "We're going until nightfall!"

Richard halted his horse. "You may have the spells you need to keep yourself together until then, but we have human needs. A good expedition paces itself, and we won't let your impatience get in the way of our respite." He followed his men dismounting from his horse, taking some bread and pieces of smoked meat from his saddlebags and leaning on a tree.

Christopher begrudgingly began to dismount. "You don't see the women complaining."

Sana snickered. "That's because I knew the constables would handle the pacing. You know men and women have different needs, right, Richard?"

The constable laughed. "You learn quite a bit growing up with nine sisters. Calm yourself, wizard, you ain't in charge of everything. You handle the boggles, and we'll keep everyone fresh and fit."

"Boggles indeed." Christopher grumbled as he began to read through his treatise on talismans. "There's no stopping a dragon, soldier, and the longer we stay here, the less of a lead we have over them!"

Richard gulped down the food in his mouth. "Why're you so sure one of those dragons is chasing us anyway? Seems like a waste to chase some people through the woods when that kind of beast could easily take down a whole city!"

Christopher frowned. "That's Haven business. Not even Judge Craven knows our full mission. Just know that when I say dragons are coming, they can arrive at any moment."

Hope suddenly looked nervous. "Wait, what was that?"

Richard chuckled. "Very funny, miss. You've got cruel timing!"

Hope cupped her hand around her ear and turned to face the sky. "No, really. It's like the wind, only... Less intense? And it's growing nearer!"

"By the powers!" Christopher slammed his book closed. "Everyone, find a place to hide! Tie up the horses and hide in the bushes!"

A look of horror consumed Sana's face. "It's finally here. These mares don't spook easy, do they, Richard?"

Richard offered a weak smile. "We train 'em not to. You could slaughter a city next to these mares, and they'd just keep munching their hay."

Christopher surveyed their surroundings intensely. "Get beneath the bushes, everyone. I'll have an enchantment to obscure its vision."

Richard nervously looked at one of his comrades as he sought the nearest bush. "Hey Harry, where's Jimmy?"

Harry shrugged. "I don't know, went out to relieve himself. Should come running back when he hears a dragon!"

Christopher growled as he began crawling underneath a bush. "If he doesn't get here this instant, he's dragon food! Hide yourselves, quickly!"

Richard was puzzled. "You can't enchant him, too?"

Christopher shook his head before retreating further. "That's not how magic works! Say a prayer for your man, he'll need it!"

Manny nestled beneath a large bush, motioning Hope to join him as he realized there was more room to hide. She soon crawled beneath the bush with him, breathing heavily in anticipation of the dragon's arrival. They stayed quiet, and Manny began to puzzle over Christopher's chosen spell as he observed no change in their environment. Christopher had called his power discernment, and Manny began to realize that he affected the discernment of others, thinking back to how his height appeared to change the night before. Looking over to the bush where Sana had hidden, Manny realized that the constable's frame had been replaced by a green blur, likely to obscure her beneath the foliage from a distance.

The sound of wings flapping grew closer and closer, and Manny began to feel the same terror he felt when hunting bears with his father. Dragons held a peculiar place in common understandings of the world. Like goblins and magic, everyone knew that they existed. Yet, they so rarely crossed paths with the civilized world that they seemed mythical. "Eat your supper, or the dragons will get you," mothers would tell their children, most knowing full well that their sons and daughters would never see one.

Manny did not know what Hope's grandfather did to keep her in line, but judging by how she still lay, he believed she was afraid. Reaching out to grab her ice-cold hand in comfort, Manny received a cold stare that soon turned to a thankful smile as color returned to Hope's face, and she squeezed his palm. *She's clutching the Dagger*, Manny realized, almost chilled by the feeling it left on Hope.

The dragon was circling now, and the travelers were startled by the distant sound of an unsheathing sword and furious running. Harry seemed to have alerted the dragon, as the well-paced flight of the beast turned into a series of quicker wing flaps sounding from his direction. It took little time for the beast to finally soar overhead, concealed by leaves and the sun's light but casting an unearthly shadow over the clearing where they were gathered.

The beast finally roared loudly, sending birds teaming toward the skies. At the same time, all manner of animals scurried toward the four winds, deer and rabbits rushing between the travelers. Just as Richard had said, the horses made no sound, even as one moved to the side to avoid the raging antlers of a fleeing elk. They soon heard Jimmy's faint cries in the distance, followed by the sound of some sort of fluid rushing from the sky. Manny knew it was too much to hope that Jimmy had drawn blood from the beast, and powerful new screams from the soldier seemed to confirm his fears.

A new roar sounded from the dragon, the screech of attack replaced by short bursts of pleasure that Manny equated to laughter. Hope squeezed his hand, and Manny attempted to comfort her with a weak smile that quickly left his face. The dragon's laughter ceased, and they heard the whooshing of its wings once again as it returned to the sky, circling above the forest in search of more prey. They heard fluid falling from the sky once again, along with the sound of drops hitting leaves and animals screaming in pain. Manny was puzzled, expecting fire to come from the dragon's mouth rather than... whatever was exiting its body.

The dragon did not fly over them again. After an eternity of waiting, they heard it fly back west, growling in apparent disappointment. Looking toward the horses, Manny was relieved to see Christopher stand up from his hiding place and motion everyone to join him. Crawling from the bushes, Manny lent a hand to Hope and pulled her to her feet, wrapping his arm around her as the travelers joined together.

Christopher breathed a sigh of relief. "I'm glad you had us rest, constable. Had we kept moving, everything would have been lost!"

Richard unsheathed his cutlass. "Everyone ain't found yet, wizard! We've got to get Jimmy! I can't I imagine what that thing did to him.

The Enchanter shook his head. "Don't go. You won't find anything left besides his sword and armor."

Richard cringe. "Well, I'm at least claiming his weapon, for his parents' sake."

Christopher continued to object, mounting his steed. "You shouldn't go anywhere near his resting place. Did you hear that raining sound?"

Richard nodded, sword still in hand. "You're not going to tell me dragon piss is cursed or something!"

Christopher's eyes rolled back into his skull. "It was venom! Dragons breathe it as fire only when they're in need of spectacle. When it's not ignited, the venom strips away leaves from trees and flesh right down to the bone. Touch a drop, and a hole will burn straight through your finger!"

Richard sighed as he sheathed his sword and walked toward his horse. "How've I never heard of this?"

Christopher laughed. "Because a dragon spitting fire is more romantic than a dragon spitting. Now, please, let's hurry on before it returns!"

Manny walked Hope to her horse. "Are you alright? I know it's following... Well, you know."

Hope nodded solemnly. "I felt it calling. Strange thing, it didn't seem to want the dragon to attack us. It was almost as though..." She stared down at it. "No, that couldn't be it."

Manny raised an eyebrow. "What?"

Hope pursed her lips. "Remember that Yukio told us a story about the dragon that rescued her from marauders in Nara? I was thinking about it for some comfort, and it's almost like... well, it thought I'd like to take a shorter trip to the Haven on the dragon's back."

Manny's head shook as he helped Hope mount her horse. "Good thing you didn't trust it. Was probably a trap."

Hope looked down at him and shrugged. "Maybe. But if it can force goblins to impale themselves on it, commanding dragons doesn't seem so unlikely."

Manny gulped. "Better be careful. It might turn on you next."

Chapter 7: Unwelcome Invaders

Hikaru and Taro walked back and forth along the parapets atop Greystone's western gate, warily surveying ragtag defenders and wondering whether they could survive the coming siege. It was a bad sign that the only attention paid by the defenders was bitter side glances, the locals feeling suspicious that any foreigners among their ranks would betray them. It likely did not help that Hikaru and Taro wore traditional Naran armor rather than poorly protected militia uniforms.

Taro could not hide his misgivings, though he was careful to speak in the Naran tongue. "Most of these men will die in the first wave. Greystone doesn't have enough men to replace them, do they?"

Hikaru shook his head. "Their numbers are too few, but the wall will hold back the goblins. All we have to fear are the dragons. If they can defeat me, the city will be overrun. If we were nearer to Legatus or one of the Deathlord strongholds, siege engines would be lining the horizon. Every scout report simply details a scattered multitude in rags with stolen weapons at best. Many have sharpened sticks or stone-tipped arrows."

Taro stopped in his tracks. "Why are we taking such an invasion force so seriously? A dragon is a true danger, but woman and children could hold against these beasts while their husbands were in the field."

Hikaru scratched his chin briefly before pointing at a nervous soldier leaning on the parapet. "M – me?" The soldier's teeth chattered. "What do you need me for?"

Hikaru smiled. "I'm here to teach. Both of you, look around at the soldiers along the wall. Cast your gaze all around the city. What do you see?"

Taro raised an eyebrow, attempting to keep his annoyance discreet. "Soldiers, prepared for war."

The soldier remained nervous. "We glitter."

Taro laughed. "Glitter?"

Hikaru smiled at the soldier. "Yes, the soldiers glitter. Every single one of you wears armor. Now, look out into the field. Notice a difference?"

The soldier answered readily, though he remained confused. "They don't glitter. No armor. We know that, though. We have a wall, and they don't."

Hikaru nodded. "So why bother at all with this siege? It's sure to be a loss, no matter how hard they fight."

The soldier finally seemed at peace. "Gives us a fright, I reckon. That's what monsters do, ain't it? Scare people. They scared me a whole bunch, most of us up here." He watched some of his surrounding soldiers nod in agreement.

Taro seemed to feel the fear that had departed from the soldier. "Goblins could only launch a siege this far away from a Deathlord stronghold if they had an immense power to control them. That's why they stay near the strongholds. No matter how monstrous their souls were, these beasts would not launch a siege on their own. Someone with dark magic has mastered the enchantments necessary to control them a thousand miles from the nearest Deathlord. And they want to flex it before the world."

The soldier gulped. "You mean there's a witch out there controlling them? Strong enough to have her own army? Do we even have a wizard nearby to fight back?" The soldier's words quickly spread down the wall, his comrades beginning to panic and buckle as the army of goblins marched closer.

Taro rolled his eyes at the fear before him, but he was quickly overcome by curiosity as Hikaru smiled and closed his eyes, nodding peacefully as he cast a spell. The mood atop the wall changed within moments, with militia appearing relaxed and focused.

"You know, I can't explain it, but I feel like it's gonna be alright." The soldier sighed.

Hikaru nodded and opened his mouth again, projecting his voice across the wall's western section. "Defenders of Greystone, fear not the coming battle. I am the Enchanter in your midst, Hikaru of Nara. I have fought a thousand battles and will fight a thousand more. Your Sheriff has placed me in command of Greystone's defense. Look to me, and I will keep your city safe."

The soldier's eyes popped. "Commander Hikaru." He nodded and vigorously shook hands. "Call me Wallace. You don't know how glad I am to have someone like you here!"

Taro smiled at Hikaru, once again speaking Naran. "I see why the Empress placed her confidence in you. One cannot simply buy goodwill like this."

Hikaru winked. "It is necessary for our survival. We must contend with two dragons and a witch if we are to deliver the city."

Wallace appeared eager. "What're your orders, commander?"

Hikaru put his hand on Wallace's shoulder. "Spread these words across the wall for me exactly, Wallace. Scouts report quite a few battering rams among the goblin horde. I expect them to spend the morning rushing the gate with their rams. Some may have shields, but they will be of wood. Archers may protect them, but their arrows will be of stone. Our armor is of steel, as are our arrows. We will be protected when they attack, and our arrows will fly farther. Those men along the wall who hunt should take the lead, firing at the attackers. If their aim is true, we can fell every goblin before they arrive at the gate. If they get that close, there will be men ready to brace it against attack, and something special currently heating in the city's furnaces. They are marching madly into a maelstrom of our making, not theirs."

Wallace saluted proudly and began to spread the word, calling groups of soldiers to his side to inform them of Hikaru's tactics. Hikaru had made his defenders feel at peace and thus more accepting of his strategy as the calm feelings faded. Now, they would be bolstered by the knowledge of a sound defense, guided by those who knew how to turn predators into prey. Militia marching up and down the wall passing by now nodded at Hikaru respectfully rather than casting their eyes away in suspicion.

Taro smiled. "I have never seen an army come together so quickly, Minister. No wonder you have won a thousand battles."

Hikaru winked again before replying in Naran. "Fought a thousand battles, Taro. Not won. And the battles I have won cost the blood of legions. I was more at ease when I could send a thousand half-breeds to die, but these men will have to do."

Taro's face contorted as he tried to maintain a smile. "And what will these men have to do?"

Hikaru shrugged. "The goblins in the hill country can climb. They spend their days among cliffsides, caverns, and trees. Survival in the hill country required adaptations that spread quickly. Greystone's wall is not porous, but it is not flat, and the goblins only need the smallest of handholds to climb upwards."

Taro could barely hide a shudder. "So we will draw our blades this morning and replace the wall's entire regiment by noon?"

Hikaru nodded. "The Sheriff did not send his best. It is easy to tell. The men around us are too old or too young to fight. Slow, fat, short, unkempt... He does not believe that the defenses will hold."

Taro frowned. "Does he not trust you?"

Hikaru shook his head. "I believe he fears the dragon that will come, as he should. In his mind, the beast will destroy his defenses and breach the gate, allowing the goblins to flood the streets and pillage the city. If he puts his best men on the wall, they will surely die first, and the goblins who follow the dragon through the gate will trample over those who remain. The men around us I sacrifice to teach him a lesson – trust me fully with the city's defense, or watch it fall."

Taro smirked. "The arrogant will always be brought to shame."

Hikaru nodded, smiling at Wallace. "That one will be the first to fall." As he delighted at the smirk on Taro's face, his ears perked up, and he realized that the siege was about to begin. "They're coming! Prepare for attack!" He drew his sword and pointed west toward the first mass of goblins approaching.

To the unprepared defenders, the goblins appeared a crazed mass, running in a scrum rather than marching in a column. They howled crazily rather than shouting or singing a battle song, with no drumbeat to guide their movements. Hikaru saw what his quaking comrades did not: a carefully manicured cyclone of terror organized by someone who knew how to make humans fear. The goblins moved in a circular mass, guarding something at their center, likely a battering ram, keeping their form in check. Only one battering ram so close to a fortification meant they knew they would not be targeted by catapults, adding credence to the theory that spies stalked the command of Greystone.

As the goblins neared the wall, several began firing arrows toward the protectors, many simply sharpened wood that bounced harmlessly off plate armor. A few protectors winced as stone-tipped arrows hit their helmets, while the first defender to fall plummeted backward onto the ground when a steel arrowhead pierced rusted chainmail. Hikaru ordered the crossbow batteries to fire arrows into the scrum now that they were in killing range, and he shortly followed with an order for the archers on the wall to begin firing at will.

Hikaru was impressed by the durability of attacking forces as the scrum before the portcullis began battering the gate, shielding itself with unexpected efficiency. Many of the goblins had picked up hardwood tabletops and metal sheets from the towns they had ravaged, expertly protecting themselves from the arrow assaults above.

"Crouch down!" Hikaru shouted at Wallace and other nearby soldiers, who nodded, knowing they would carry the message. "Archers, get down! We'll brace the gate while you rest. Save your strength for the next wave."

Taro tapped Hikaru on the shoulder and pointed at the sight of wagons approaching with steaming cauldrons. "They'll enjoy this surprise."

Hikaru smirked as blacksmiths hurriedly marched up the wall steps with cauldrons of molten sand. He hid a laugh as he listened to the emboldened goblins howl at the men bracing the gate they desperately struck. Once the smiths gathered atop the rampart, they began flinging the torturous waste onto the invaders, taking little time to work the beasts into a frenzy. It only took a few to become so irritated that they dropped their shields and danced around wildly to remove the melting flecks from their rags and armor, leaving their comrades undefended for similar treatment. The entire scrum was dancing around wildly within minutes, scattered and defenseless.

"Archers! To your bows!" Hikaru shouted, and the order went out again, defenders firing their missiles into the crowd with zeal. The sound of laughter nearly matched the dreadful row of monsters in the field, and that began to change the mood. As the molten sand finally cooled and fell away, goblins began to pick up their fallen weapons and regroup, forming clusters and making a dash toward the wall.

"Swords ready!" Hikaru raised his sword in his hand in a fighting posture, Taro following as the command went out along the wall again. He was dismayed to realize that many brought old hatchets and even large cutlery to the wall as defensive weapons, cursing the Sheriff's timidity. Only Wallace had a real sword, though its ornamental finery meant it would likely shatter against better weapons.

The archers grew weary as they continued firing arrows at increasingly manic and ferocious goblins, several taking hits and running with greater vigor to decimate their foes. Shouts of fear began to sound as goblins began springing onto the wall and climbing, building hives that allowed their comrades to ascend more quickly. Fighting along the ramparts broke out quickly, and Hikaru realized the wall would be overrun before reinforcements arrived. Hikaru had intended to allow a massacre atop the wall to teach the Sheriff a lesson, but he realized he would look ineffective if he did not cast a spell to end the fighting.

"Taro! Snap and slice!" Hikaru shouted at Taro, who leaped away from a group of goblins he had been dueling and waited for his master to intervene. Hikaru closed his eyes and cast out his hand in a balled fist, casting an enchantment to freeze the nerves in each goblin's spine. The five Taro had fought were paralyzed, and Taro quickly dispatched them. They tossed the bodies over the wall and watched the goblins respond by moving further down to avoid the foes who had bested them.

An eternity seemed to pass as Hikaru flooded the wall in a river of carnage, thinking back to his years of study of goblin anatomy and casting spells to pinch nerves, snap tendons, and break bones. It was tedious but horrifying, shocking the defenders as they beheld the true potential of magic while the goblins merely responded to stimulus and adapted by moving rather than fleeing. Looking up at the sun through scattered clouds, Hikaru estimated that an hour had passed by the time he destroyed the goblin horde. He and Taro leaned back on pillars and rested, finding jugs of water rapidly placed in their hands as they closed their eyes and rested. Once they finally looked up, Hikaru smirked at the site of the battered defenders along the wall kneeling before him one by one, captivated by the greatest display of magic in a generation.

Hikaru's pride was cut short when something in the distance caught his eye, and he tapped Taro before pointing in the distance. The goblins waved a white flag, a symbol that a higher power among them knew the time and manner for negotiating. He ordered a white flag be raised along the wall to mark a moment of peace before making his way to the Sheriff's Citadel. The time had come to meet the Skurlag character – but first, the Sheriff needed to learn that his failure would not be tolerated.

The Sheriff shouted when Hikaru slammed a severed hand on his desk, prompting loud knocks on his office door where he had offered Hikaru a private meeting. Despite Hikaru's scowl, Juan assured worried subordinates who knocked on his door that there was no cause for alarm before he settled back and nervously toyed with his mustache.

Hikaru remained angry. "You know why I brought you this, don't you?"

Juan cringed. "You wanted to show me that my best men aren't enough, and we need to prepare better for the dragons."

"Best men! I-" Hikaru held back from shouting before laughing aloud. "Don't lie to me, Sheriff! That motley rabble of old hunters and schoolboys was doomed from the start. You don't trust me to defend your city, and that's why you held your best men back!"

Juan defiantly rose from his chair and stared directly into Hikaru's eyes, conviction matching rage. "I ordered my best men to the wall. I don't want a single civilian in this city to die. If my best men weren't on the wall, then someone countermanded my orders. And that person needs to be locked in my dungeon at once!"

Hikaru scratched his chin as he and the Sheriff continued their showdown, realizing that Juan spoke from a place of genuine conviction. The Sheriff was an immigrant himself, once looked upon as a foreigner like Hikaru. There was no reason for him to be so mistrusting. They both knew that the militia had been infiltrated by people who sought the talisman in Hope's possession. Their continuing deception stifled Greystone's defense and divided its commanders.

Hikaru finally relented. "How would you like an opportunity to demand a fair fight from our attackers?"

Juan raised an eyebrow. "Demand a fair fight? You can't reason with monsters!"

Hikaru shrugged. "True, but you can reason with the power that controls them. I came here because the goblins raised a white flag. They wish to negotiate. Before you dismiss it as absurd, consider that we can engage with the intelligence commanding our attackers."

Juan appeared to relax. "If you think it wise, I will join you in negotiating with the attacker. But this time, I will handpick everyone who joins us."

An hour later, Hikaru and Juan rode down the highway from the western gate in a small party of soldiers, proudly flying the banner of the Republic. As they rode forward, two hundred soldiers exited the city and stood in formation beyond the gate, while their better-trained comrades took over positions on the wall. Within minutes of navigating the road through the hills, the riders came face to face with a band of goblins. Hikaru was especially unnerved to see their white flag up close, a blood-stained wedding dress.

Sheriff Alonso was defiant. "We see you've decided to surrender! We welcome your decision. Take us to your leader."

"Hardly!" The only goblin wearing a fitted suit of armor waved his hands, and the monsters around him stood still. "Cut the chatter. You have something we want. Give it to us, or we'll destroy Greystone."

Sheriff Alonso rolled his eyes. "We haven't a trinket you mongrels would fancy. You've seen how far your battering rams have gotten against our defenses. None of you will stand a chance in our city!"

The goblin laughed slowly. "And here I thought you wouldn't allow us to test our metal. Very well. Fire!"

As arrows met their target in every member of the party, Hikaru suddenly found himself the lone rider left atop his horse, startled stallions scattering away in terror only to be pulled to the ground and torn up by famished goblins. Sheriff Alonso alone seemed to have survived the arrow wound to his gut. As he weakly attempted to stand up, a goblin forcefully jammed the butt of his spear onto the wound.

The armored goblin laughed. "He'll make for sport tonight. We won't break ground until you return to your soldiers, elf. I want them to know the name of Skurlag before the ground breaks and their city is taken from them."

Hikaru began to raise his hands and conjure a spell, but he reluctantly stopped himself as the Sheriff shook his head. He was right, Hikaru decided, turning his horse to gallop back toward the city. They needed an enchanter for when dragons flew over and the ground... Broke! He kicked his horse to ride faster as he moved toward the city, hoping to warn the soldiers to get back into the city before they were swallowed up by the terrors beneath their feet.

By the time he arrived at the gate, Hikaru saw two hundred young men cut down instantly. He had seen dreadful routings before, but a superior force's decimation of an army remained shocking. There was no way to warn the men as he rode toward the wall, though he at least tried to alert them by frantically waving his arms. This did nothing to prepare them, however, as a dozen massive wyrms shot up from the ground and displaced the bodies around them.

Multiple soldiers were grabbed in the mouths of their attackers, who rose up twenty feet in the air and dropped them back onto the ground, some impaled on the spears of their comrades. The soldiers on the ground did their best to fight back, finding more luck in piercing straight through the wyrm skins rather than slashing. Crossbow batteries on the wall successfully pinned down two wyrms, fiery darts lighting the flammable oil secreted from their skin. But in the end, the giant, gray monsters had decimated the force below, bodies strewn about after being dropped from on high or smashed through as the wyrms burrowed through the loosened soil.

This was the endgame, Hikaru realized, thankful to arrive at the gate just as the last wyrm returned to its place below the ground. He was hurriedly let back inside the gate, ranking officers desperate to understand the depth of the trouble they had encountered.

Hikaru waved his sword. "Get everyone on the wall! Anyone who stays on the ground is dead!"

Taro was the first to respond. "Where's the Sheriff?"

Hikaru panted. "He's gone. I'll explain more on the wall! Run, you fools!"

Wallace began spreading the word. "Replace the barricade and get back on the wall!"

Hikaru shook his head, dismounting his horse before running up to the parapet as quickly as possible. "Leave the barricade, it's no use!" His senses were immediately overwhelmed by an onslaught of approaching goblins, swarming the plains and hills as they howled to the heavens. Little time would pass before they rushed the gate. Hikaru feared the wyrms would demolish the entrance, leaving the city vulnerable to swarming goblins.

Beneath the parapet, a roar of exploding stone followed by shouts and screams confirmed Hikaru's suspicions. The defenders below were vanquished, and the gate creaked open, soon to permit the free flow of goblins into Greystone.

Hikaru needed the men to show caution. "Crossbowmen, wait until you can see the eyes of your targets! Every man with a spear, join me at the stairs and impale these beasts! Prepare your swords for war, everyone else. "

The soldiers around Hikaru prepared to follow his orders. A few dropped large stones onto the ground behind the wall, and when a wyrm arose where it heard that movement, Hikaru's comrades filled it with spears and arrows. The wyrm began to scream, disappearing below ground to recuperate. Spears and arrow shafts in its side splintered loudly against the tunnel as the goblins that made it past the crossbow batteries finally arrived inside the city.

The first warriors with their feet on the ground, Hikaru and Taro began leaving piles of bodies strewn all over the ruptured streets. Their position did not hold for long, as the inexperienced young men around them were forced back into the city or onto the wall. Hikaru was relieved to see a column of heavily armed lancers with shields approach but realized too late that the wyrms would come for them. While these soldiers were better prepared to fight than the battalion that had evaporated outside the wall, they left their fight with the wyrm too few in number to stem the tide of goblins.

Guiding the survivors to the top of the wall, he whispered a thankful prayer at the arrival of archers from nearby positions, who deftly cut through the crowd of invaders below. Hikaru's men quickly cut down those goblins who tried to climb the stairs themselves, but he knew they could not hold their position forever. The fields outside the wall were quickly filling up with masses of goblin archers who were able to cut down defenders simply due to the volume of arrows they launched. Looking around town, Hikaru could see towers and homes shaking as wyrms followed vibrations in search of prey to devour. So long as they held the ground hostage, the wyrms could keep reinforcements in the city from reaching the wall, allowing goblins free reign to enter the city.

Hikaru's fear only visibly manifested when he saw smoke rise from the Hirose Hotel, perhaps due to a tremor knocking a loose candle to the ground. The Hotel would likely be evacuated, and the occupants spilling into the courtyard would surely draw attention from one of the wyrms.

Taro began to panic. "Minister! The Hotel!" He stabbed a goblin through the chest and kicked it to the ground. "Go! I will take care of the wall."

Hikaru nodded, proud to see one of his proteges leading. In between careful lunges forward at approaching enemies, Hikaru looked around to see buildings across the city begin shaking together as though the wyrms were speeding toward the Hotel. The faces of his retinue flashed before his eyes, and Hikaru recalled the vow he made to protect Lauren and Varsha.

Looking out at the goblin crowd below the stairs, Hikaru balled his fist and stretched out his arm, feeling a will to strike down the invaders so that his wards could be saved. Without warning, the goblins who made it past the wall suddenly dropped their weapons, black eyes transforming into a milky white as boils began to cover their skin, and their lifeless forms fell to the ground. It had been ages since he had stricken so large a force, and he was thankful that magic could turn the tide.

Taro nodded his thanks as their fellow defenders cheered at the slight reprieve. "Go, now! They need you!" He slapped Hikaru on the shoulder before brandishing his sword at a new group of goblins warily peaking through the gate at their decimated comrades.

Hikaru ran down the stairs and dashed toward the Hotel, staying close to the buildings and praying that he would not be grabbed by a stray wyrm. The ground became more unstable the closer he came to the Hotel, pieces of the gate hanging on hinges due to the subterranean ruptures. Peeking between them, he was baffled by the sight of wyrms lazily drilling up and down through the ground, frightening a scattered rabble of horses loosed from the Hotel's corral. He counted the ten surviving wyrms from the gate, leisurely gobbling up the sweet soil that had caused the surrounding gardens to blossom into a garden of Naran plants.

As the wyrms grew more lethargic, guards from the Hotel took advantage of their sloth to launch an attack. Several stood near the courtyard's edges firing flaming arrows, while others rode unsaddled horses into the mass of spontaneous flesh arches, puncturing skin with poisoned spears. The engorged wyrms eventually met their end, and the ground again felt peaceful. Marching through the courtyard, Hikaru disregarded the defenders alighting wyrm carcasses and marched straight into the foyer, shocked to find Christopher's wards with Yukio.

Hikaru was livid. "What are they doing down here?"

Varsha smirked. "Oh, we were brushing horses when a fire started in their corral, and they had to be rushed out. Brought the wyrms right here, but that wasn't much of a problem after all, was it?"

Hikaru's eyelids shook as he stared Yukio in the eyes. "I told you not to let them leave the Hotel! Those things would have eaten my wards, and the blood would have been on your head!"

Lauren put up her hands in protest. "Please, sir, we asked her to go outside!"

Hikaru frowned. "So my assistant cowered to the demands of witless youth? Such insubordination deserves the punishment she will receive."

Yukio nodded in submission, aware that her disobedience had likely earned her removal from his retinue and the dishonor that would follow. "My lord, I accept the consequences of my actions."

Hikaru nodded. "Your quick repentance is appreciated, but your penance shall be long. Now get back to your-"

"Hey, that's no way to thank us!" Varsha's smug expression remained. "The wyrms are all gone because of us. Now you can go back to defending the gate!"

Hikaru was taken aback. "What do you mean? I ordered you to stay inside! The wyrms were not some curse punishing you for leaving your rooms!"

Varsha rolled her eyes. "Oh, come on, old buddy. You don't think the wyrms randomly made their way here, do you? If not for me and Lauren, they'd still be tearing this city apart!"

Hikaru squinted, then turned his face to Lauren. "Your friend speaks in riddles, young lady. Clarify."

Lauren cringed. "Well, Varsha's good with animals, and I've read a lot. She came up with the idea of getting the wyrms in one place to eat because, well... That's just their nature. She even knew how to get them here, by causing a stampede."

Hikaru was unimpressed. "A clever guess that was more likely to get you both killed. Why did you think the wyrms would stay once the horses scattered?"

Lauren blushed, and she spoke when Varsha nudged her. "I read one of the books in the hotel library about horticulture in Nara. And I thought back to another book I read a long time ago about the giant wyrms in Cimmaron. The composition of the soil from Nara, transported to grow the plants outside, matches remarkably with a giant wyrm's ideal diet."

Hikaru turned to Yukio, doubting Lauren's story. "She read that entire book this morning?"

Yukio shrugged. "Minister, she read five books this morning. I've never seen anyone read so fast. Or remember so well."

Hikaru raised an eyebrow. "You read five books in half a day, memorized them, cross-referenced them with something else you read before, and used this knowledge to a clew of wyrms?"

Lauren smiled weakly. "We did it together. We just... I mean, Varsha prodded me, but we both wanted to help. There were so many people screaming..." She shook fearfully.

Hikaru slumped back and wiped his brow. "With skills like that, you belong at a Haven. Would you consider staying there rather than returning to Braddock?" He knew their return home was unlikely, but now that he saw potential in them, the two girls seemed destined to wield the Great Powers. "Lauren, you have the mind of a Professor. And Varsha, few Rangers can boast to have killed so many monsters, especially not in their first battle."

Lauren blushed again while Varsha beamed proudly. "See, I knew you'd come around! And we'll be right here to help when the dragons come."

Hikaru shook his head. "I was planning on burying you underground when the dragons arrived. But you've given me pause." He turned to Yukio, who remained anxious about her final judgment. "You should be discharged immediately for disregarding my orders. And you would be, if these two hadn't defeated the wyrms as they claim. But now we need to put their claims to the test. Join me at the Courthouse this evening to meet with Judge Craven." He turned and left Yukio in doubt, giving her one last chance to prove her value.

Judge Craven was still distraught over the Sheriff's capture when Hikaru visited him after a day of fighting. "The City is lost! We prepared for goblins. We didn't prepare for wyrms. And we could never prepare for a dragon! Without an

Enchanter, we'd be doomed…" He hobbled over from his desk to a liquor cabinet to pour himself a stiff drink.

Hikaru was grave, planning to share sterner words with the Judge while Yukio and his wards waited outside of his office. "The wyrms did a great deal of damage. Nobody could have expected that they would travel so far from Cimmaron. That they are here signifies that we face a far more powerful enemy than a common witch."

The Judge tried to hand Hikaru a glass but put it back down when it was refused. "Minister, I should have listened to your friend. Maybe we'd be safer if those two young ladies went with him. The goblins would have passed us by while we stayed locked up here. Let the Haven handle the monsters."

Hikaru shook his head. "Thinking about what might have been at a time like this is a distraction. To the goblins, it's just little fish grinding their teeth. But after rain falls, the ground hardens. We destroyed their great surprise weapons, and we filled in the tunnels the wyrms made. The gate was barricaded, and we have now likely killed more than half of the monsters outside. Until the dragon arrives, they'll be pushing curtains with arms."

Judge Craven squinted as he sat back down at his desk. "I'm sure that idiom means something in Nara, but platitudes won't help when a dragon finishes my city! Greystone is several square miles in size. How can we possibly defend against these creatures?"

Hikaru winked. "I told you before, I've killed hundreds of dragons. And it was a complete fabrication." He allowed the Judge to gasp. "It always takes a team to bring down a dragon. And I have led armies to slay hundreds. They are truly terrifying creatures, and far more powerful Enchanters and warriors than I have met their end in dragonfire. We must plan soon and prepare our forces with the expectation that the dragon will arrive tomorrow. I'll need you to sanction my… command staff, as it were, to kill the monster."

Judge Craven raised an eyebrow. "From among your diplomatic retinue, I presume?"

Hikaru nodded and called for the doors to be opened, Yukio and his wards entering shortly after. "Judge, my assistant, Yukio. And two of the young ladies we were escorting to the Haven."

Judge Craven's head shook. "You're going to kill a dragon with... them?"

Hikaru laughed as the three new entrants were taken aback. "Yukio, you brought a vial of dragon venom with you, right? From your dragon?"

The Judge spat whiskey back into his glass. "Her dragon! Don't tell me you keep them as pets in Nara!"

Yukio shook her head. "No, Judge. Not as pets. But the dragons of Nara are at peace with the people, unlike in Manifest and Nova. And yes, Minister, I have a vial."

Varsha snapped her fingers. "Well, we've got all we need to kill a dragon! Assuming we still have some archers and lancers left?"

Hikaru nodded.

Varsha smiled widely. "Yukio, you said that dragons like patterns, right? So, we use that venom to make a pattern. If we can somehow sprinkle it around the city, we can get it to a place where it will be easier for warriors to bring down and dispatch! Lauren, what do you think?"

Lauren looked up at a stylized painting of Greystone mounted on the wall behind Judge Craven. "We dip arrows in the venom. Not a lot, but enough that the dragon can smell it when they whiz by or strike it. And we set the arrows in a pattern. A circle around town, perhaps. Then we let it spiral until it's been hit enough times that it falls to the center of the city to lick its wounds, and it can be captured there."

Judge Craven laughed. "Captured? By the powers, we're going to kill it! Mount its head on the western gate for the goblins to howl at! If this plan works, of course. Minister, you've killed dragons before. Really think it'll work?"

Hikaru nodded. "I'm learning not to underestimate these young ladies. I've never killed a dragon quite like this, but it stands a good chance. Dragons are attracted to each other, and we often bring their venom when we need to hunt them. And while their scales are tough to pierce, they tire easily if struck in flight. It takes a lot of muscle for them to stay in the skies, and those muscles are fatigued when attacked. It will work."

The Judge finally smiled. "Seems like something you are capable of organizing, Minister. But what do we do once it's down?"

This was the easy part for Hikaru. "Cover it in hot tar, then drop rocks on it. The beast will be too weighed down to move if you can do it quickly. It will flail at first, but there should be a few places in the city where this will work. Once immobile, a sword through each eye will do the trick."

"And a dragon tooth for each of us!" Varsha's exclamation drew the Judge's ire. "Hey, I like to take a trophy from all my kills. This wolf fang is getting a little musty." She pulled a necklace from her bodice and held it up for the Judge to see."

The Judge was taken aback. "The women of Braddock must read from a different copy of the Feminine Virtues. A constable, a hunter, a talisman wielder... Perhaps you should be teaching in our schools!"

Lauren smiled. "I'm going to attend the National Academy. Maybe I should study to become a teacher while I'm there."

The Judge chuckled. "I should think you'd be a better fit for the Haven Academy if it stays open. And if we survive this all, an intellect like yours could be invaluable to me in Red Hall."

Lauren gasped. "So you are running for President! And... golly, yes sir, your honor. It would be a privilege to work in Red Hall!"

The Judge grew reserved once again. "Only if we survive. If Hikaru is wrong to place his trust in you, the people of this town will be buried together, and Greystone will just be a stain on the map. I trust you now because I have faith and nowhere else to turn."

Hikaru nodded. "So it must be the right course of action. Even if it rains or spears fall, Judge, we do what is best for your people. And for the world." Hikaru's final words mystified his companions, but he knew they would fight harder for Greystone if they understood the battle's true stakes.

Chapter 8: Unwelcome Ghosts

"Can someone tell a story before we go to bed?" Hope was fatigued after a long day of riding, and she felt some cheer was needed after the close encounter with the dragon. The party had been unnerved by the soldier's death earlier, especially his comrades, and Hope knew they needed something to get their minds off the tragedy.

Christopher shook his head. "I think it's best if we all got some rest. We'll be up before the sun, and we'll need all the sleep we can get."

Perhaps the setting is all wrong, Hope thought. Their makeshift camp was a haphazard mess, spread out over a small clearing with nothing to keep them centered. Worried that they would invite enemies, Christopher had forbidden a fire, and they had chosen to randomly place their bedrolls.

Sana nodded in agreement, the prolific storyteller crushing Hope's dreams that anything would be done to raise some cheer before they slept.

Christopher finished removing his robe and sash and looked over at Sana. "Do you still want to take the first watch?"

Sana nodded again. "I can stay up late but won't wake up earlier than needed. This is just my speed."

"Right." Christopher nodded and resumed his preparations for bed.

Hope saw an opening. "Sana, if I stay up with you, are you sure you can't tell a story or two? I need to get something else in my head after today."

Constable Richard grumbled, already lying on his bedroll. "Heh, we all do, missy."

Sana chuckled. "I can't keep watch if you're watching my tales in your head, little girl. Let us have some peace tonight, yeah?"

Hope looked to Manny for some emotional support but found the youth already fast asleep, having disappeared quietly into the realm of dreams. Defeated, Hope crawled onto her bedroll and tightly wound her cloak around her frame, clamping her eyes down and praying for a peaceful night. She tried to think of a serene sight to placate her troubled mind, settling finally on a peaceful farm like she had seen outside Greystone.

Braddock was high in the hills, surrounded by trees that were logged and sent away, not the wide open wheat fields she had glimpsed around Greystone. Even in the dim morning light, the carefully managed plains had evinced a certain serenity she tried to recall. She sank ever deeply into the vision of grain spreading for miles, swaying in the breeze under a bright blue sky without a care in the world.

Thoughts turned to dreams, and Hope envisioned herself a toddler lazing on a wooden porch surveying the fields, snacking on blueberries, and drinking lemonade as the warm sun comforted her. Hope became vaguely aware of company, glancing up at a smiling man and woman, the latter holding an infant in her arms. They seemed to be the portrait of contentment, the quintessential farmers of Manifest, keeping the hungry fed in a world of lurking dangers.

The smiling woman looked down at her. "Hope, mustn't leave the porch."

But why shouldn't I? Hope thought. *Such a beautiful summer day...*

The smiling couple entered the house, and Hope seized her chance to leave the porch, scooping up handfuls of rich soil and rubbing them in between her fingers. The specs of dirt soon turned to dust, floating upward only to darken the sky with menacing clouds that blotted out the sun and poured forth heavy rain. The wheat stalks quivered and cried out in pain as the rain turned to hail, and they were cut down, making a path for an encroaching army of goblins. Hope tried to yell a warning as she scurried back to the porch but could only clamor in fearful cries, failing to form a single word.

An armored figure burst through the farmhouse door and leaped from the porch, brandishing a broadsword and large shield. The figure was met in the field by goblins, savaging several of them before their numbers became overpowering. Their helmet was ripped away, revealing the courageous face of the woman who earlier held the infant in her hands. Arrows fired from within the farmhouse allowed her to continue fighting again, but they could not overcome the flood of goblins that continued to trample the fields in pursuit of the warrior.

Soon, a painful cry from within the house was followed by the last defending arrow, and the woman was pushed to the ground. She smiled weakly at the porch before defiantly facing the menacing blades of her captors one last time. Fear filled Hope's heart as the goblins turned to the porch and lunged forward, ready to share the warrior's fate with her family.

"Gina!" A familiar voice rang out as a horde of human reinforcements approached the farmhouse. Soldiers on horseback slashed through the attacking goblins, many of whom ran away in fear only to be vaporized by lightning and fire from the staffs of two enchanters. The lead rider who had called out the name of the fallen warrior jumped from his horse and held the woman in his arms, weeping and crying out in pain.

"She was the last one." An enchanter patted the rider's shoulder in comfort as he addressed other rescue party members. Their faces became clearer, Hope recognizing the lead rider as her grandfather, while the Enchanters manifested as Christopher and Flora alongside Lauren's late uncle Daniel.

In a dark twist, they seemed to pass Hope by on the porch as they entered the house and searched for survivors. It was her fault, leaving the porch only to invite darkness and death, and she resolved never to question authority again if she were rescued.

"I'm here!" Hope tried to call out. "I'm alive!" Nothing but the cries of an infant sounded at first, but Hope continued shouting until she found herself exclaiming the words in the middle of the clearing. "I'm here! I'm alive!"

"Quiet, Kathryn!" Sana's bizarre directive shocked Hope out of her cries.

"Ugh..." Hope breathed heavily while adrenaline surged through her veins. "Sana? Are you awake?"

"Huh - what?" Sana seemed to snap awake from the tree where she had apparently fallen asleep, jumping up to visit Hope. "What's wrong? You sound like you've seen a ghost!"

Hope sighed. "I... I had a dream. An unwelcome dream. I've had too many of them since I awoke from... that long slumber, after Dead Falls."

Sana huffed. "Argh, what I wouldn't give for a pill to calm you down. Take a few deep breaths and try to steady yourself. I'll be right here, just, I don't know, think of happy thoughts and clear your head."

"Right." Hope was thankful that she was not alone, as indifferent as the company was. "Happy thoughts..." Neglecting the wide open fields, she recalled Braddock's deciduous trees turning green in the spring, spreading cheer throughout the forest. How grand they always looked, seen from hills around the town, the brown and gray veins finally vanishing from the emerald woods...

Sana seemed to sense when Hope's breathing returned to normal. "Feeling better now?"

Hope sighed. "Yes, thanks. I'm glad I wasn't alone."

Sana chuckled dryly, clearly unhappy to deal with such an annoyance so late at night. "Just don't make a habit of it."

"By the way, who was Kathryn?"

It was difficult to see the color likely draining from the constable's face, but Hope heard her gasp loud and clear. "How do you know that name?"

Hope was surprised by the acrimony. "You shouted it right as I awoke. Don't you remember?"

Sana groaned and left Hope's side. "Forget you heard that. Get back to your nightmares, and I'll get back to mine."

A convivial energy had flowed through Hope's veins the moment she espied the looming spires of Trumaria. Occasionally running her fingers around the hilt of the Dagger, she found that the talisman almost fancied their arrival as a sort of homecoming, and she began to receive impressions of dormant memories tied to passing monuments and towers. Impressions almost grew to whispers, the very same carnal uttering that had filled Hope's mind during the goblin attack at Dead Falls. Despite compounding into an odd sense of comfort, Hope guessed that the Dagger's communications were deviant at best. Sooner or later, they would overpower her will. Still, Hope was scared to reveal her troubles to Christopher, merely a distant acquaintance of her grandfather. All she could do was pray that her resistance held out long enough to arrive in Angela's Haven, where the magic of the Enchantress could melt away her troubles.

Manny spoke up as their route through the forest took them closer to the ruins. "We'll not go along the main highway into town. It's probably got the most goblins, even at this time of day."

Richard agreed. "Lad's probably right. We're in for trouble whichever way we go, but we can succeed if we sneak in where they least expect us."

Christopher smiled proudly. "We're in your hands now, Manny."

Manny gulped in worry as Christopher's words drove home the weight of his responsibility.

Smile.

At the Dagger's prompting, the curve of Hope's lips into a joyful expression returned the color to Manny's face, and he confidently led the party forward into the unknown wasteland of Trumaria. They needed a confident leader, but Hope suspected for the first time that the will of her unwelcome talisman might be leading them toward a darker destiny. The dark spirit within was sure to lead them into ruin, wielding the uncertainty of promised dishonesty and the terror of unpleasant truth equally in a battle for dominance.

The party marveled at nine centuries of unrestricted growth that had given plants dominance over the ancient cityscape, transforming towers into trees and avenues into meadows. Feats of engineering that defied known science had propelled these towers into the sky, blocking sunlight and emboldening the cold. Crossing the intersections between the old city blocks left the party vulnerable to chilly blasts of air, and Hope wished she had a warm hand to hold amid the cold. But alas, the horses were too far away from each other, and the hand she most sought to hold had been engrossed in conversation with an Enchanter. Between Sana's cold stare and the brutish quiet of the soldiers, the remaining options for interaction were undesirable, so she found her hand grabbing the Dagger's hilt once more.

Envious that the two could socialize, Hope moved her horse forward to at least hear Manny and Christopher talk. She knew Christopher was screening the young man for fitness as an Enchanter, a demanding career that left little time for attachments. Hope grew evermore intrigued by Manny, and she worried that he would be snatched away into a solitary life before they had a chance to explore their connection. It was not unheard of for miracle workers to hone and practice their gifts outside the Haven. Still, it was unlikely that Manny would go down that path for the sake of a girl so soon after fulfilling what seemed to be a fervant dream of training at Angela's Haven.

Manny seemed to be more excited as they drew closer to Angela's Haven. "You know, one thing I won't miss is the clothing. As the Sheriff's son, my clothes were proud and garish, and I've never loved it. But the outfit of an Enchanter - oh, how I admired the simplicity! Long, dark coats and tall, wide-brimmed hats, their dignity signified by that pure, white collar..."

Christopher laughed. "I never could stand those hats. I always felt dragged into a web of pure solemnity. Byeong has quite a sense of style - the robe and sash are simple, yet the colors are fun and free! Dark red robes to remind us that we're serious, and umber sashes to let people know that we are safe. And we shave our heads to avoid drawing further attention to our worldly appearance."

Manny chuckled. "The difference in dress between Enchanters on each continent has always fascinated me. Every Haven sends a message with its uniform about the way they interact with the divine. I should hope to visit all of them one day, just like you!"

Christopher was pleased to be a role model. "You know, it is not so common as you'd think for an Enchanter to visit every Haven; at most, we visit the other on our continent. I may be one of the few humans to visit every Haven in a lifetime - and this dedication to collaboration has had its rewards."

Manny nodded vigorously. "I heard before your election no one thought it possible that an Enchanter from one Haven would go on to lead another. The *National Courier* stopped its negative attacks on the Havens for a while to commend the spread of continental values outside Manifest."

Christopher sighed. "Something dark had seized the heart of the Republic's leaders. Twenty years ago, your people saw trade and cultural exchange as the means of achieving peace and power. Now, the Roots Party, the Society of Virtue, and their 'free' churches instruct your press and politicians to attack allies and old friends to preserve superiority. That's why I had to leave."

Manny was equally glum. "Tis certainly a pity. Even Judge Craven thinks it's possible that he could lose his enough office in due time."

Christopher remained anxious. "Well, as an Enchanter, you can leave that all behind - assuming we survive our journey through Trumaria."

The Enchanter's doubt chilled Hope to the bone, reintroducing the fear she had felt under the dragon's shadow. Surrounded by an infinite number of goblin hideouts, Hope understood how even an unseen enemy could project fear. Her heart rate elevated as she began to peer closer at her surroundings, worried that every unexplained movement in the corner of her eye was an enemy waiting to strike. Sana and the soldiers seemed equally unnerved, turning from vigilance only to cast fleeting glares at Christopher for revealing their location with his speech.

Hope caught her horse up to Sana. "Do you think we'll be alright?"

"Only if we keep quiet."

Hope sighed at the constable's uncordial brevity. "Right..."

The constable continued to confound at every turn, almost driving Hope mad as she attempted to discern Sana's true identity. She recalled a thousand stories Sana had told, all positing an impossible timeline for a human yet described with eye-catching detail... And now this Kathryn? The mysterious name, called out in the dark, had betrayed a strong, matronly connection, perhaps to a daughter or young sister. She might have been the one person to have given Sana true joy, only to be ripped away in a moment of tragedy.

Hours passed as they made their way through the city, the sun barely growing in warmth as they passed through the forest of steel and stone. Boredom grew exponentially over time as Hope grew tired of listening to Christopher and Manny drone on about the minutiae of life in a Haven. She finally found some respite when Richard called the party to stop as they approached what may have been an overgrown park.

Manny was unnerved by the suggestion. "We should keep moving? We can't afford to lose any time if we're to make it out of here before dark."

Richard was dismissive. "We need to keep up our strength in case we've got to flee goblins later. Especially the horses. It's half an hour til noon; we'll move on when the sun is midway through its day."

Before Manny could continue his conversation with the Enchanter, Hope stole him away and asked him about their conversation. "Sounds like you and Christopher are getting to know each other quite well. Are you enjoying yourself?"

Manny's smile consumed his face. "Oh yes, I've learned so much already! He's absolutely brilliant! Did you know that Havens have their own islands in the middle of the oceans, shrouded by magic and discoverable only by enchantment? Sounds like the perfect place to relax after a quest!"

"Is that so?" Hope was annoyed that Manny had not noticed her being within earshot of the pair throughout the ride. "You Enchanters almost seem like you're on an island of your own."

Manny was confused by Hope's irritation. "Hey, at least you'd had Sana to talk to."

Hope shook her head. "She's only said a few words this whole journey. I don't expect her to be talkative any time soon." Manny shrugged. "Well, perhaps you could get her to tell you a story."

Hope pursed her lips. "Ugh, you don't understand. Despite the company, I'm alone for the first time in my life. The horseback ride is too uneven to read or sew. I'm stuck with my thoughts, and whatever interesting tidbits reach my ear from your talks with Christopher."

Manny frowned. "You could hear that? I thought we were being private!"

Hope chuckled dryly. "I'm always surprised by what people think others don't hear. You've talked about a great deal, so tell me, how does it all make you feel?"

The frown on Manny's face turned into a smile. "Feel? Well, it's so interesting, what he tells me about -"

"Interesting is not a feeling." Hope was insistent. "Manny, you're leaving your father behind for a world you know absolutely nothing about! How does that sensation work through your heart?"

Manny took a deep breath. "Well, it's exhilarating. Like the first time diving into a river from a cliff. The ground has fallen out from under me, and I don't know when I'll hit the water or how it'll feel, but I'm not afraid of what I'll find."

Hope was impressed by Manny's poetry. "And how does your father come into the picture?"

Manny thought for a moment. "Suppose it's like leaving solid ground. Though, maybe not quite as solid as my father supposes."

"How do you mean?"

"Well..." Manny looked off into the distance. "It's not easy to explain."

Hope smiled. "I'm here to listen."

"I guess, I'd say... We don't have matching tastes. And he's not interested in hearing what I have to say."

"What, does he turn you out when you bring up a book you read?"

"No, it's not quite that bad." Manny sighed. "His response is more vague. When I bring up something that intrigues me, his eyes seem to glaze over, and he turns away at the earliest convenience. How am I supposed to be taken seriously, complaining about so muted a response?"

Hope nodded. "I could see how easily it would be dismissed."

Manny's solemnity remained. "I wouldn't even know how to bring it up, anyway. He works so hard for others and takes such good care of me, it would seem rude to fault him for so small a thing. But I can't help feeling despair that he shies away whenever I bear my true heart."

Hope smiled again, wishing that his anxiety would depart. "I imagine talking with Christopher is like coming up for air, then. I'm glad that you've been given this chance. But you've got one more opportunity to see your father before you enroll in the Haven - will you keep this from him?"

"Eh, why bother with what goodwill we still have? Like I said, he's been a splendid dad otherwise. I don't want our last memory to be defined by bitterness."

"Won't it just grow over time if you don't deal with it?"

Manny snapped. "It's too late, and that's that! I... Sorry. It's just - I've never had anyone to discuss this before. I even kept it from my best friend; Benjamin and the Judge seem to get along so well, I can't imagine they'd have a problem like this."

Hope nodded. "Apology accepted. My grandfather raised me, and I had even less to share with him. Seems like he understands me less over time!"

Manny smiled wryly. "I can only imagine wanting to know someone like you more over time.

Bat your eyelashes.

"Oh, just shut up!" Hope groaned, suddenly pulling her fingers away from the Dagger's hilt.

Manny peered down at her side. "Does that... That thing talk to you?"

Hope looked at the ground. "I wish it didn't. Don't tell Christopher; I don't want him to think I have a problem. Angela will make it better, once we arrive at the Haven."

Manny nodded. "I promise. I know that's not really a part of you. You're more than just the girl who found the Dagger of the Locu-" Manny suddenly put his hands over his mouth. "I mean, the talisman. Whatever it is. It's more-"

Hope's eyes widened. "What did you call this thing?" She looked down at the Dagger with revulsion.

Manny cringed. "Sorry, I think – it's um – a story. Yeah, it's a story. One that I've been telling myself. You know, to pass the time. That you've found the greatest weapon of all. And, uh, you'll save the world with this quest we're on." He smiled weakly.

Hope turned to try and catch Christopher's eyes so that Manny's awkward rumblings would be made clear, but she was surprised by what she found. "Strike me, did everyone take a nap? And where are Sana and Christopher..."

Manny was worried. "Gone to relieve themselves – or – wait, what's that in Richard's neck?" He gasped in horror. "It can't be! Onto the horses!" Manny leaped toward his steed only for it to whinny weakly and fall to the ground. Terrified, he grabbed Hope in his arms and dragged them both to the ground, wearily shielding his face.

Hope was terrified. "Is it goblins?"

"Shh!'"

Deep in the undergrowth, Hope heard the clang of steel swords followed by wicked goblin howls. A fireball appeared in an alley down the road, followed by a hasty Christopher shouting and waving. The Enchanter arrived in the clearing just as Sana finally vacated the forest, panting while brandishing her cutlass.

Christopher's eyes were crazed. "We can't stay here! We're almost completely surrounded. Split up!"

Sana shook her head. "Split up? You need to tell us where we're going!"

Manny tried to protest. "Southeast to the River, but we can't split –"

"It's the only way!" Christopher grabbed a reluctant Manny, running behind a nearby tower.

Sana spat. "Hell-spawn." She grabbed Hope's hand and began running in the opposite direction.

Hope tried to speak as the sudden sprinting made her lose breath. "Yeah, these goblins are horrid!"

Sana laughed. "No, The Enchanter."

"Please, can we stop now? I can't bear to run another step, I mean it." Hope stopped in her tracks for what seemed the first time in hours and bent over with her hands on her knees, panting in discomfort as large raindrops pelted her back.

"The goblins haven't got tired, believe me." Sana moved forward without acknowledging Hope's fatigue. "I wanted to make it to the river before darkness, but it might as well be evening with this storm. Keep moving!"

"At least let me get out of the rain for a few minutes!" Disinterested in Sana's opinion, Hope walked to the nearest building and opened the door, warily surveying the inside before entering. It seemed to be an ancient market, shelves and glass cases lining the walls covered in deteriorated goods left behind by the Skyborne centuries prior. The building was somehow marked by a solemn peace that Hope expected Sana to interrupt at any moment, though she was determined to enjoy her moment of rest while it lasted.

Walking through the shelves to the other side of the store, Hope found a counter similarly furnished with unrecognizable clutter from times past, all adjacent to a slightly open door. Something about the entrance made her uneasy, and just as she turned to leave, the door creaked open wider. What little light came through the building's glass doors eerily aligned through the door, and Hope gasped at the sight of a dark-haired older woman in a white dress lying on a bed.

The woman waved her forward. "Come closer, my child. I haven't seen you in some time."

Something about the woman drew Hope closer, and she began to recognize the face from her dream about the toddler on the farm.

The woman sat up and allowed Hope to join her atop a white throw. "Right here, nothing to worry about. You can trust your mother."

"Mother!" Hope was taken aback at first, but the comforting gaze of the impossible woman with a face from a dream led her to relax. "It is you. It really was you, in the dream."

The woman nodded, a chilly hand stroking Hope's hair. "Yes, the Dream. You heard me, calling out to you. And it's all thanks to that." She pointed at the Dagger, which Hope was not surprised to find herself nervously clutching again. She did not know the woman but felt a sense of familiarity that she wanted to keep by her side. "You must come with me, then. We're leaving the city."

The woman sternly shook her head. "Nonsense, my child, stay with me. It's perfectly safe. A girl must have a mother, and now we shan't leave each other's side."

Hope felt urgent. "Well, I can't stay here forever; I'm on the run." The woman stared blankly, not accepting Hope's excuse. "I mean, I've got a life to live outside. School to finish, boys to meet if I'm to get married-"

The woman angrily grabbed Hope's wrist. "Why get married? Isn't your mother enough for you?"

Hope's wrist chafed as she unsuccessfully tried to pull away, and she was thankful to hear crashing glass outside just as she felt an impulse to grab the Dagger. Sana barreled through, brandishing her sword at the woman and summoning Hope to her side.

"Come closer, my mother, I haven't seen you in a long time." With a glimmer of light, the woman's form changed into something smaller, her face transforming into one Hope could not recognize, and she jumped from the bed in horror.

Hope finally understood what they were facing. "Sana, run! It's a ghost!"

"Kathryn?" Sana began to tremble at the sight of the woman who had claimed to be Hope's mother.

The woman smirked. "Right here, there's nothing to worry about. Don't you trust your daughter?"

Before Sana could move, Hope tugged on her arm but found competition from the woman, leaving an uncharacteristically indecisive Sana stuck in the middle.

"It's not really her!" Hope shouted, finding that she was losing the battle. Once Sana had finally lurched forward, Hope looked down in despair and felt the Dagger's prompting. Manny's odd slip about it being the Locust's talisman felt oddly validated, and she felt she had some measure of power over the ghostly woman. Summoning every ounce of strength in her body, Hope unsheathed the Dagger and lunged between Sana and the woman, plunging the blade into the latter's heart and shouting for it to leave. Sana jumped up in surprise, knocked from her trance as the woman screamed and exploded into a dazzling ball of light.

"I'm free!" The woman's voice emanated throughout the room from nowhere in particular, and within a moment, the storm outside grew fiercer.

Sana leaned against the wall and growled. "Hope, don't you dare wander off like that again! It took all my strength to find a way through the barrier, and next time-"

"All your strength? It was just glass!"

Sana shook her head. "Skyborne glass is like nothing I've seen. It's a miracle I could get in here at all."

Hope looked out at the hideous storm visible through the broken glass. "Maybe we should stay the night here if it's that difficult to get inside?"

Sana shrugged. "We've got as much a chance in here as out there. But at least we'll be dry. Besides, your dark magic seems to have rid this place of predators for the time being."

Hope gulped at Sana's accusation of demonic power, angry at first but soon horrified that perhaps she was becoming an evil being trapped in a body that would one day celebrate death. If this was indeed the Dagger of the Locust, as Manny had accidentally revealed, she would morph into the most evil spirit of all

Sana was blissfully unoccupied with thoughts of the arcane, settling on the bed without regard for its old inhabitant. Hope hesitated to join her, fearing some latent enchantment in the shop that would carry her further down the path to witchcraft than possessing the Dagger already foretold. If she closed her eyes, perhaps the Dagger would take hold of her...

"I think I'll take the floor." Hope did not want Sana to worry about her increasingly unpredictable nature.

Sana yawned drowsily. "Suit yourself, Ka – kid. But don't be afraid to dream up here when your back gets sore."

Chapter 9: Unwelcome Dragons

Hikaru enjoyed his final moments of morning peace with Judge Craven and Taro eating breakfast in the Courthouse. The Judge seemed at ease enough about the city's prospects that he had avoided alcohol since the night before, guzzling coffee to stay alert. He knew exactly how to show hospitality to a foreign leader, an ideal candidate to become the Republic's next President.

Judge Craven finally took a break from eating. "So, what do we know of this Skurlag character? I've never met a dark magician before, and they haven't caused problems in this country in living memory. Should we expect that Juan made it through the night?"

Hikaru did not wish to ruin the Judge's mood. "All we can do is pray that he survived. But there is something at work in this siege that makes me think our dark magician would be bored by simple murder. They will want to send a message with the Sheriff's fate. We must focus on the dragon now so vanquishing it overshadows Juan's destiny, however dark."

Taro had not warmed to Hikaru's trust in Lauren and Varsha. "Reinforcements better get here soon, the plan to take down that beast is worrisome. And I know you've killed more dragons than I, Minister, but only the Empire and the Haven have the weapons we need to slay one."

Judge Craven chuckled. "Your Minister is not just an experienced warrior, young man. He's an Enchanter. Where weapons fail, magic will succeed. Just ask the goblins outside. They'd be mindless marauders in the woods without their… Skurlag taking charge. Just as we'd be overrun with monsters if Hikaru hadn't been able to command both men and magic."

Taro frowned. "I'm a hundred years older than you'll live to be, Judge. I know what it takes to kill a dragon. The plan is not impossible, but there are more certain tactics to pursue."

Judge Craven shrugged. "Nevertheless, it is the plan devised by citizens of the Republic, so it is the plan that must deliver our victory. We cannot rely on magic alone."

Hikaru nodded. "Magic was not intended as a weapon. We know a bow will fire. We don't know that a miracle is the will of the divine."

Judge Craven sighed happily. "Your work at the gate has miraculously driven up our morale. Our men never dreamed we'd have an Enchanter at our backs, much less leading the charge."

Hikaru remained humble. "I am but a channel for the wisdom who wields that power. If it stands with us, we can strike down the dragon. But as Taro said, the best thing to happen is for the Haven or the Empire to arrive first."

Judge Craven frowned. "Governor Deas better return quickly. Sending him across the ruins of Trumaria was not one of my brightest decisions. We would stand a better chance with two Enchanters among our ranks. The political calculus remains unchanged: the Havens rescued Greystone from a siege. There is nothing like war to make you question whether you made the right choice. The only bright spot in this battle is that two of our young women will best a dragon."

Hikaru shook his head. "Your city would have been safer had you allowed me and Christopher's other wards to journey with him. This siege would have been avoided entirely."

Judge Craven was livid. "Bottle your disappointment! I'm the elected leader of this county, and I did what was best for my city. It was, ultimately, insurance that Christopher would return like he promised."

Hikaru began to groan, then suddenly found himself grimacing in pain, his ears shutting out the sound of a dragon screaming outside. Unable to similarly protect his ears, Judge Craven clamped his hands over the sides of his head, falling to the ground. Unmolested by the sound, Hikaru ordered Taro to tend to the Judge while he ran onto the office deck, looking out over the town square to see a dragon flying above the city. It continued screeching for some time, pausing only to shower venom onto buildings and exposed people in the streets. Little time would pass before the dragon lit its venom, setting buildings all over Greystone ablaze. Howls in the distance alerted Hikaru to a new wave of goblin attacks, likely returning to the western gate but perhaps emboldened now to strike all around the city.

He could only watch and pray that the archers and lancers followed the plan. The dragon's flying was haphazard until it saw a plume of green smoke lit on the north side of town as part of a planned diversion. The dragon roared when arrows hit it and quickly rained fire on the building below. But it moved to the east soon after, howling again when arrows hit it and then flying to the southeast.

Hikaru was less surprised that the plan worked than he was worried by the prowess Christopher's wards displayed. Hope carrying a Deathlord's talisman without growing feral was a curious feat on its own, but having two best friends who instinctually knew how to defeat both wyrms and dragons… That was too random to be a coincidence, and Hikaru came to terms with the fact that Christopher was hiding something.

The dragon lunged onto a tower nearer to the center of town and spent a great deal of time tearing the roof apart. Distant screams from defenders barely made their way to Hikaru's ears, and he worried that the beast had come to sense a deadly pattern. As it jumped in the air and spread its wings to fly away, Hikaru closed his eyes and spread out his hand to conjure a boil in the middle of its wing, causing the dragon to lurch in the right direction. It thundered onto the top of the Haven Cathedral, weakly pulling itself up to scratch the lesion that appeared just far enough along its wing to make scratching difficult. Enraged that it could not alleviate the pain, the beast took to the air once more, seeking venom to alight but finding itself again drawn to the arrows and spears with another dragon's fluid.

Battles like this inspired awe in historians, but not the dead, and even less so in the survivors who would panic every time they relived the carnage. It was the type of spectacle that the great Caleb Defoe had brought to life in his many annals of world history. Now, his own progeny was responsible for starting a war that would puzzle historians for some time to come, provided the secret of the Dagger could be kept. A man with such an eye on the mechanics of the past understood the future better than anyone else. Hikaru began to hypothesize that Christopher's three wards had a unique destiny that would be revealed now that they had been loosed upon the world.

"By the powers, it's finally down!" Judge Craven slowly approached the deck, rubbing his ears. "How soon till it gets back up?"

Hikaru shook out of his thoughts and looked down at the town square below where the dragon had finally collapsed, convulsing as it licked its wounds. "Never, if we get the boiling tar and stones in time. Alert the man stationed on the decks above the square to begin their attack, and send in a squadron of lancers you don't mind losing.

Judge Craven nodded. "At once! The men in the buildings will look to the Courthouse to know when to move."

Watching the square below, Hikaru marveled at the green-scaled dragon, thirty-foot body and ten-foot tail spread out beneath decorative awnings. Its left wing was splayed along the ground, skin blistered and free of scales after it had apparently grazed a few buildings in an attempt to scratch the boil. With its right front leg, the dragon had pulled the damaged wing toward its mouth, helplessly seeking relief by licking the wound. Hikaru smirked as he looked up and saw the buildings around the square silently fill with men.

Aroused by the smell of burning oil, the dragon quickly arose from the awning and pushed itself away, smashing the support columns of the awnings above. It attempted to move toward the middle of the square, only to be met by two dozen lancers with steel shields. Unable to breathe fire after spending its fuel on buildings, the dragon roared and moved back toward another awning, finding itself once again surprised by molten tar pouring from several windows coordinated by Taro. The dragon roared, attempting to stand on its hind legs before soldiers began pelting it with tar-soaked rocks.

The beast soon fell to the ground, weighed down by the burden of increasingly heavy stones on its body. A squadron of cavalry soon arrived, and Hikaru nodded in approval as they planted their spears in the ground to anchor strong chords that were slung across the dragon's quivering frame. Once the beast had been subdued, Hikaru and Judge Craven walked into the square and stared it in the face, Taro joining them to observe his handiwork.

The Judge was impressed. "You really were a true threat to the dragon, Minister. The plan of attack may have come from your wards, but we have you to thank for coordinating the assault."

Hikaru nodded. "Dragons are easier to kill when they've fallen from the sky. I learned that one about eight hundred years ago. Would you like to do the honors, Judge? Then you can truthfully say the dragon was killed by a citizen of the Republic."

Judge Craven smirked. "Aye, when I hang its head above the square where it fell, no one will dare attack my city again!"

"Then you'll need another sword." Hikaru handed over his own blade. "Men, help me secure it!" He ordered some nearby soldiers to help Taro press down on the beast's snout to hold it still.

"Where do I strike the killing blow?"

"One sword through each eye."

Whenever he had seen a dragon die this way, Hikaru noticed how well it seemed to mimic the emotion of terror, petitioning its final foes for mercy. Like many a half-breed he had executed for stealing food and water from regular troops in the War of Four Emperors, Hikaru knew to ignore the plea of an abomination. While the Judge hesitated upon drinking in the doomed beast's expression, Hikaru shoved Craven's arms forward. In a final show of strength, the dragon threw Hikaru and the Judge back before slumping down one last time.

"For Skurlag." The muted final roar sputtered from its throat. "For Skurlag." Its eyes turned to glass, and the sword blades snapped in half, falling to the ground.

A nearby soldier laughed when Judge Craven displayed a look of abject horror at the killing. "What's the matter? Not like it's your first kill, right Judge?"

The Judge slumped, and his face turned white. "No." His nostrils flared, and his eyes wavered as he glared at Hikaru. "My first murder."

Manny was surprised that goblins had not accosted him for the remainder of the journey through Trumaria. Christopher suggested that the goblins had been drawn to the Dagger, voicing regret that he had split up the survivors rather than protect them from what darkness lay ahead for Hope. They prayed that Hope had not been overtaken by enemies but feared to go back and search for them. All they could do was head to the river, which Manny had described to Sana as the ultimate destination for their journey. The riverbank could be followed from early morning until late afternoon before a boat from one of the towns downstream took them to Angela's Haven.

They waited on what looked like the remains of an ancient dock all night, keeping watch and hoping they had not traveled too far away to find Hope and Sana the following day. A thousand evils plagued the city, and Christopher suggested that Hope's loss within would finally draw Angela to destroy the ancient ruins in a desperate search for the Dagger. Thankfully, the morning brought a surprise boatman, who paddled toward shore when he saw Christopher and Manny waving their arms. Dropping anchor, the boatman set forth in a dinghy to approach his newfound passengers.

"The hell you doing in these parts?" The elder sailor invited the newcomers onto his craft. "Nobody survives a walk through Trumaria!"

Christopher smirked. "We're no ordinary people. Christopher of Byeong's Haven, at your service."

"And my name's Manny, I'm from Greystone."

The sailor laughed. "A wizard and a city boy, extraordinary indeed. What brings you to these parts? Haven business?"

Christopher nodded. "Can you be of further help to us?"

"How do you mean?"

Christopher tried to remain gregarious despite the weight of his request. "We've got two companions we expect to be making their way to the shore at any time, might already be here. Can you sail up and down the river for a while and help us search?" Seeing a frown on the sailor's face, he acted quickly. "Angela's Haven will reward you handsomely."

The sailor scratched his chin. "You don't look like one of them wizards from Angela's Haven. There's smoke rising from Greystone, and everybody's under suspicion, so tell me what you're doing, or I'll sink this boat right now!"

Manuel shook his head anxiously. "No, we're a warning party seeking aid from Angela. My name is Manuel, son of Sheriff Juan Alonso. If you don't take us to the Haven, the blood of Greystone's children will be on your head!"

The sailor chuckled as they came alongside his boat. "Well, now I know where to send the bill. Up you go!"

Once aboard, the sailor handed a lengthy pole to each of them and began barking orders. "Time to get pushing! This boat's not gonna take itself upriver!"

Christopher was aghast. "Pardon me, I'm in no shape to do...whatever this is!"

The sailor rolled his eyes. "Suppose you're ready to swim back to shore then?" The sailor laughed, shoving the pole into Christopher's hand and forcing him to drop his staff to the ground. "This boat's not gonna keel itself upriver!"

Christopher begrudgingly dug the pole deep into the water, and Manny was quickly obliged to follow suit. After a couple hours on the boat, Manny was sure his arms would fall from his shoulders, consumed by the giant, amphibious lizards he saw lazing near the shore. Manny could smell nets full of freshly caught fish within the small lean-to on the ship. He was propelled forward by no greater thought than to empty the fisherman's catch in the shore and roast what he could in a fire set upon the city ruins. Christopher appeared truly unwell, finally passing out from exhaustion after an hour, but quickly revived by a splash of water from the fisherman. The old man kindly allowed Christopher to consume nearly a gallon of his supply before getting him back into the rhythm.

On their first trip back down the river, Manny was relieved to see Hope and Sana near the dock area. Sana kept them further on shore, as far away as possible from the ravenous lizards in the water. As they moved closer, Hope was the first to turn and shout, waving her hands to alert the boat's unknown occupants. While Sana was hesitant to join, she soon waved her hands as well, which Manny attributed to the sight of Christopher's red cloak.

Manny lifted up his pole and shouted gleefully. "That's them!"

"Oh, thank God!" Christopher removed his pole from the river and slumped to the ground. "I couldn't move this pole another inch!"

The sailor began to drop anchor. "Sure, you can rest a spell. But it's two hours more to Perry Ford, and I'm not forcing a lady to do a man's work here." He laughed at Christopher's replying groan, and Manny began to worry for Christopher's safety. While Christopher was much younger than the sailor, Manny knew the latter's muscles were built up after years of navigating the craft.

Once Hope and Sana had boarded, Manny noticed a crucial difference in reactions, the former excited be out of danger, and the latter ready to execute Christopher. The Enchanter expected a frosty greeting, acknowledging the danger in which he had left his ward and her guardian, but he was not prepared to be savaged.

Sana yanked Christopher by the collar. "If you ever run away from us like that again, I will kill you where you stand! We were almost taken by a demon in that city, and we had a life's fill of avoiding goblin traps! Our survival is a miracle, and if we ever get out of here, I'm throwing you to the courts for leaving us in danger!"

"But there's no extradition treaty with your country-" Christopher tried to protest before Sana quickly interrupted. "I know."

Christopher pulled back as Sana let go of his collar. "At least we searched for you when we found a boat. I've practically broken my arms moving these poles around!"

Sana shook her head and picked up the downed pole near Christopher's feet. "Probably because you weren't doing it right. Go ahead and sleep. We'll take care of everything from here."

The sailor finally returned the anchor to the ship. "No man comes aboard my ship without doing his fair share. But if you want to join us, ma'am, well, that'd be mighty good of you. Might get us to Perry Ford half an hour earlier."

As Christopher tried to protest returning to work, Sana shifted her eyes warily across the ship. "Where's the rest of your crew, captain? This is a four-man sloop, at least."

The sailor stammered. "Oh, um... They're... Up the river. Spending a few days away from town and all. I'll take back a larger crew and boat to pick them up in a few days."

Hope had surreptitiously entered the lean-to on deck, alerting everyone to her whereabouts with a shocked cry and holding open the blanket covering the entrance. "What large oysters!" Within the structure were several nets full of the plate-sized shellfish Manny recognized as Perry Oysters, a staple in wealthy homes throughout the Republic.

Sana was livid at the sailor. "Where did you get those? You shouldn't be this far up a restricted waterway, much less taking oysters back! Why, they'll contaminate the rest of the oysters you'll ship!"

"The rest?" The sailor stuttered in confusion. "Yes, the rest. The rest of the oysters from Perry. The... The ones that will ship to the rest of the... country..." He seemed to understand that his continued stammering only grew Sana's suspicions of foul play. "Look, ma'am, oysters is oysters, whither we get them. I understand this young man is the Sheriff's son and guess you're in his employ too, but lay off a moment. Seems you had a long night running through the old city, and I'm surprised you're not mad after all that. Take a moment and consider the favor I can do for you, being here after all, and think about if you really just thought you saw my haul as the result of some dark magic or poisoned spores."

Manny grew annoyed at the standoff as he found himself pushing the boat further through the water by himself. "At the very least, help me pilot this thing!" In response, Sana dipped her pole into the water and expertly began moving the boat forward while the sailor fetched a fourth pole for Christopher.

Hope tried to diffuse the situation. "Can I help at all?" She smiled cheerfully as she eyed a pole.

The sailor shook his head anxiously. "Thank you kindly, young lady, but I've got us all the help we need. Just be ready to fetch water when we get thirsty."

Sana begrudgingly went back to keeling. "What's your name, sailor?"

The sailor gulped. "Oh, uh, call me Arnie."

Sana smirked. "Right, Arnie, I'll think good and hard about whether I've been seeing things. The longer it takes us to get to Perry Ford, the less patience I'll have for your poaching."

Arnie gulped, and Manny hoped Sana's loyalty would not get them stranded on the river without a proper captain. Though the constable seemed to be a practiced keel-hauler, there was no way a woman who had spent her adult life in the mountains possessed the skill necessary to sail to Angela's Haven.

Manny decided to jump at the chance to interact with Hope more. "Mind if I have some water?"

"Right away!" Hope gleefully quickly rummaged around the deck to find a cup before delivering refreshment.

Manny sighed deeply after a few gulps. "Ah, magnificent." Hope still appeared as beautiful as she had the day they met, fiery red hair and green eyes shining atop the stained, tattered dress and cloak that had barely kept her dry through the storm. He expected he would grow more thirsty as they sailed down the river, and he would savor every drop of water Hope brought.

Christopher groaned at the sight of a fishing village. "Oh, thank goodness, I couldn't go any further! Is that Perry Ford?"

Sana decided to needle the fisherman. "More importantly, is that the place where Perry Oysters really come from?"

Arnie frowned. "Like I tried to say, don't ask the question, and we won't need to speak of this ever again."

Hope realized it was not only his secret to hide, remembering other boats that had passed them going up and down the river over the last couple of hours. She vaguely recalled Varsha bragging about her mother procuring some of the shellfish a few years prior, but they had not become so popular that the poor knew them as staples of a wealthy table. Most curious was Sana's suspicion of criminal activity, which she had never associated with the simple act of fishing.

Sana decided to remove her pole from the water and lean on it. "I've got a story to tell. Years ago, I came to the Republic as a deserter from the New Airgiallan army. My credentials placed me in a pair of constable boots not long after immigrating here, and one of my first cases involved black market smuggling in Yorkton."

Christopher huffed. "Fascinating! We're nearly there, Sana; maybe spare the story until we're rested?"

Sana dismissed him with a laugh. "I'll save the details, but I remember the smugglers were doing something nobody expected. They used humble fishing boats from reputable establishments to ship untaxed alcohol through the city. Everyone thought the dockyards for the Fishermen's Union were above board and that trust kept constables from going inside. At least, until someone without regard for their sanctity burst in with a warrant and busted the whole operation."

Arnie appeared nervous even after hours of keel-hauling through strong currents and other dangers. "You don't say?"

Sana shrugged. "Never caught the chap who ran the joint. A fellow named Arnold Tyrel. I'd sure fancy running into him again."

"That's... That's not the way they tell it!" Arnie cowered back from his shout as Sana raised an eyebrow. "At least not in the papers. At the time. It was thirty years ago, after all. Who really remembers?"

Sana winked. "Well, Arnie, I remember it perfectly. Those old leathery uniforms were miserable on a hot day, I felt like I was glued into my trousers!"

"No, no, it can't be!" Arnie dropped his pole in the water and stumbled backward, shocked as though he suddenly remembered Sana's face. "Are... Are you her daughter, ma'am? Is she still alive? Oh please, don't tell that woman I'm still alive! She'll have the courts put me away for sure! And I've got families depending on me-"

"Relax." Sana was calm, gently returning her pole back to the water. "I just wanted to make sure you didn't send someone a bill for transporting your cargo."

Arnie wiped his brow with a handkerchief. "Discretion is priceless. Now that I think about it, young lady, you look rather like your mother. Tell me, is she still alive?"

Sana winked again. "Oh, the constable who took down your old operation is alive and well."

Arnie gulped, suspicious of Sana's identical appearance. "Well, I wish her all the best."

Hope attempted to ease tension in the boat. "I've never had a Perry Oyster; might we have some for lunch?"

"What? Those fetch fifty dollars apiece-" Arnie stopped short due to Sana's glare. "I mean, sure, one or two for each of you couldn't hurt. It's not like there won't be more of them."

"Hey, do you all hear that?" Manny peered west toward the shore. "Like a windstorm or something."

Arnie shrugged. "Happens all the time, cyclone out on the ocean."

Manny shook his head and worriedly looked toward the eastern sky. "No, it's over the forest!"

Hope cried aloud in fear at the sight of a massive dragon hurtling through the sky, crying loudly as it flapped its wings and dove toward Perry Ford. Fire gaped from its mouth like a waterfall, and clouds of smoke from its nostrils blotted out the sky.

Arnie's eyes popped. "By the powers! Turn back, now!"

Christopher placed his pole back on the boat. "We're not going anywhere!" Lifting up his staff, he closed his eyes and muttered a short prayer followed by an illusion of the river swelling near the town. "Drop anchor! Get ready take me to shore!" He expanded the illusion to raising waves that danced, drawing the dragon's attention. Determined to show its superiority, the dragon flew straight toward one of Christopher's waves and blew a white-hot flame into the center, evaporating the illusion.

Hope was terrified, running to squeeze Manny's welcome hand and crazily running her fingers around the Dagger's hilt. This was it - this was the city brought to its knees under dragon fire, all because Hope had brought the a dark magician's talisman into its midst. She had fought goblins and unfaithful humans with ease, but a dragon was a true foe, and the talisman's owner would want more than anything for the Dagger to be taken by a monster of great power.

"Get her off the ship!" Christopher shouted as the dragon flew toward them.

Arnie's crazily shook his head. "There's no running now! We're dead!"

Christopher was defiant. "That beast will know the death of fire before it takes us! Brace yourselves!" He conjured the illusion of his staff shooting a fireball at the dragon, which made the beast role in the sky so forcefully to dodge it that it strained a wing. It screamed in pain and flew much higher into the air temporarily, waiting for the pain to disappear.

The Enchanter turned to Arnie. "Take my pole, get us to shore!" Arnie nodded and ran to take Christopher's place, jamming his pole into the water as quickly as possible. Thanks to the pain of Christopher's spell, the dragon stayed in the air long enough to allow them to reach the docks. Sana immediately put Hope and Manny to work evacuating the village while Christopher stood firm on the pier, brandishing his staff in defiance of the dragon circling overhead.

Manny's head was clear, the result of his father's training. "Where are we going?"

Sana scanned the horizon. "Send them southeast. We'll run as fast as we can towards the Haven." She disappeared into the village, knocking on doors and spreading the word of the plan to the villagers.

Hope ran to the nearest door and peered inside a shack, dismayed by the sight of a young woman rocking back and forth with an infant.

"You need to run!" Hope waved her arm frantically, but the woman did nothing, rocking back and forth as though she was alone.

Frustrated, Hope's hand slid to the hilt of the Dagger, and she began to feel a tingle in her eyes. "Flee for her life." Hope's command came directly from the Dagger, and its words resonated enough for the woman to get up and run, bowing in valediction.

Outside the shack, Hope saw Manny attempting to herd a group of young boys carrying sticks and wood sheets. Moving toward the crowd, Hope realized Manny was losing an argument to leave the village. One of the boys finally whacked

Manny on the head with a stick, and as he staggered away, Hope watched them foolishly run towards the docks.

Standing in the middle of the alleyway, Hope slid her hand around the hilt of the Dagger once again, eyes tingling. The youths stopped in their tracks and seemed to cower at the sight of Hope.

She smiled wryly. "Run to the Haven with your family. They need your protection in the woods." The boys nodded obediently and excitedly ran to the edge of the village to fulfill their mandate.

Manny approached cautiously, eyes locked on her face. "Hope? Are you alright?"

Hope snarled at his doubts. "Get back to evacuating!" Looking down, she realized that her hand still clutched the Dagger's hilt, and she hastily pulled away.

Manny pointed to the southeastern sky. "There's something in the distance."

Hope grimaced. "Another dragon?"

Manny shook his head. "Not this time. Airships, from the Haven!"

Hope smiled. "Tell Sana to run to them." She left while Manny searched for the constable. Turning toward the river, Hope was horrified to see the dragon swooping back down to the docks. The beast screamed, and Hope fell to the ground in pain, head throbbing from the piercing cry. Christopher too was knocked down, and the dragon flew over him, reaching down its tail to grab the Enchanter from the ground and carry him through the air, dropping him into the river.

There was no surprise when Hope felt her hand slip toward the Dagger, and this time, she welcomed the tingling behind her pupils. Running toward the docks, she stood firm and drew the Dagger from its sheath, raising and pointing it at the dragon. Apparently curious, the dragon flew toward her on the docks, landing behind Hope and blocking her access to the village. Walking right up to the beast, Hope stared directly into the dragon's eyes as it sized up the prey before it.

Hope almost coughed as she breathed in the stench of smoke orbiting the beast, barely keeping her composure as she imagined being crushed between its jaws. Dark red scales shimmered brightly in the sunlight, coloring what could be her final sight with dancing hues of blue and purple. The world stopped for a moment as her eyes were consumed with those colors.

You know what I am.

Hope shook her head, refusing to entertain Manny's fearful slip of the tongue the day before.

The boy named me.

Hope shivered. *I don't want it to be true.*

The Dagger's tone shifted humorously. *And I don't want my new host to be killed by a dragon. Follow my lead once more.*

Frozen solid with fear, Hope's vision returned with the tingling behind her eyes, the Dagger taking control once more. "Stop! Destroy them first." Her hand was raised in the air, pointing southeast toward the approaching airships. The dragon sniffed loudly in disapproval but jumped into the air all the same, flapping wings blowing Hope to the ground as they carried the beast toward the sky. Breathing heavily, Hope lay on the ground in shock, barely absorbing the gravity of her interaction with her pursuer, the cause of all her fears and this journey to the Haven. Had she stayed in Braddock, could she simply have waved the dragons away?

"Hope!" Christopher clamored from the water, alerting her to the sound of the Enchanter swimming toward the dock. Hope got up and looked down at Christopher as he slowly made his way through the water. When he got to the pier, she reached down and helped pull him up, only for the Enchanter to sit down and take deep breaths.

After he had rested for a moment, Christopher chattered a question. "Was it the Dagger? Dragons don't just run away from an easy meal."

Hope hung her head. "Yes. It was drawn to it, but when I wrapped my hand about the hilt, it spoke through me. That's the voice the dragon heard."

"That doesn't follow." Christopher raised an eyebrow. "Not based on what we know. You should be ash swirling into the wind as that dragon carries the Dagger away to the Loc – I mean, its owner."

"About that…" Hope searched for the right words, despairing at Christopher's imagery and imagining that the dragon intended to finish the job if it defeated the airships. "It told me what it is, who it really belongs to. Does - does this mean I'm a witch?"

Christopher hesitated. "Hope, we don't know nearly enough about the Dagger to say anything for sure. All I know is that you saved a village from a dragon attack, a legendary feat on its own." He patted her on the back, attempting to comfort her following his vague deflection. "Now let's watch the Haven do their work."

After telling Sana to head toward the airships, Manny ran back toward the docks to find Hope. His courage failed when he saw the dragon descend in the distance, but he found some solace when the beast returned to the skies without the sound of flames flaring. He did not know if Hope was hurt, but at the very least, he could hold her hand in her final moments.

In the distant skies, Manny could see the dragon approach a pair of airships, dark and subdued compared to their opponent's flashy exterior shimmering in the afternoon sun. He could watch the beast tear the airships to shreds in time, he decided - Hope needed a hand to hold. Arriving at the docks, he was relieved to see Hope sitting next to a soaking-wet Christopher, who had removed his sash and outer robe as he shivered from the lingering river chill.

"Manny!" Hope exclaimed. "Has everyone left?"

"Yes." Manny nodded, anxiously awaiting the Enchanter to jump into action. "Just pray they'll reach the Haven before the dragon gets them. Christopher, can you protect them?"

Christopher chuckled. "You underestimate the Haven. Relax a minute, young ones, and watch a dragon meet its end."

Shrugging, Manny nervously sat beside Hope and let his legs hang over the dock, a foot above the choppy water. High in the sky, the dragon's flapping wings appeared to disturb the path of the airships, turbulent winds shaking them. Undeterred, the airships staid the course, marching through the air together but parting as they came within range of their enemy.

Thinking to find one easy target, the dragon flew toward an airship on its left, only to find harpoons from both vessels spring forth into its flesh. The dragon roared loudly in pain, then began to flail around, breathing fire at the cables attached to the harpoons. Manny was surprised to see the cables light up in a brilliant flame, likely soaked in hot oil before being shot forth. The flames terrified the dragon, which struggled all the more but soon found itself exhausted. As the beast's movements slowed, the airships began to circle it in a dance, wrapping the flaming chords around the beast and arousing fresh howls.

Remembering the times he had hunted bears and wolves with his father, Manny expected that the dragon would not go down so tamely. Fighting for its life, the beast bent its long neck toward its left side and wrapped its jaws around one of the extended harpoon arms. Screaming loudly, it appeared to excrete the remaining saliva from its glands, weakening the metal harpoon rod so it could be snapped in half.

Christopher gulped, quickly standing. "That bodes poorly. Let's make our way to the Haven, shall we?" The Enchanter briskly walked down the dock while Manny jumped up and helped lift Hope from her seat.

As he followed the Enchanter, Manny looked toward the sky again and saw the dragon continue to fight, letting forth a mighty but more subdued scream as it wrapped its claws around the harpoon lodged in its hide. Within a moment, it succeeded in pulling the harpoon free, only for blood to rain onto the forest below. The beast seemed to swing toward the other airship hooked via harpoon, only to swing backward. Relieved momentarily that the airship remained intact, Manny realized that the creature was going exactly where it intended, swinging back and forth so that it could get closer to the other craft. Its moment increased over a few swings when it finally moved far enough to launch the harpoon from its claws into the other airship, piercing the canvas covering with a loud pop and hiss.

Immediately, the airship began to descend, and Manny feared for the people in the woods who were potentially threatened by the falling wreckage. He looked forward into the woods for a moment when they finally reached the edge of the village, intending to avoid seeing the terrible crash for as long as possible.

"Look!" Hope tugged at Manny's arm and pointed to the sky. "Think they'll make it?"

Manny looked up again, surprised to see dozens of human bodies jump out of the falling aircraft. Most allowed themselves to fall, while a small group appeared to propel themselves forward, gliding through the sky in suits with cloth outstretched between their arms and legs. Each held a lance, razor metal glinting in the sunlight as they soared through the air toward their prey. The dragon attempted to swing away from his new foes, avoiding the first one to come near it, only to scream in pain as a second adversary glided above the beast and allowed himself to fall straight down, lance finding its mark.

Finally subdued, the dragon's body merely shuddered as the next few gliders impaled their enemy, and eventually, it hung down like a rock for a moment before the airship detached the harpoon cable. Manny's stomach turned as he heard the whine of the beast falling through the air, landing on the trees below with a great crash and the din of splintering wood, followed by a great cloud of dust and leaves.

Christopher suddenly turned, waving at Manny and Hope. "Back to town. We'll have them land in the water and take us forward." As he scurried forward, he lifted his staff in the air, a bright light emanating forth to alert the remaining airship to his presence. Accordingly, the airship began to move through the air towards Perry Ford, gradually descending until it lowered onto the water beside the dock and hung an anchor. A gangway was extended from the airship cabin onto the pier, and a man in a dark green ranger's cloak stepped out to wave Christopher and his companions forward. A party of elves within the airship cabin greeted Christopher warmly, one quickly handing the Enchanter a cloak to warm his shivering body while dwarfs and humans expeditiously scurried about the space.

"Christopher, good to see you again!" The Enchanter was greeted by an elf in a dark coat with bizarre spectacles, missing collar betraying him as a Professor.

"Kandar!" Christopher vigorously shook his comrade's hand. "I was worried I'd miss you on my visit."

Kandar laughed. "If we hadn't seen that dragon in time, you might have been roasted before we could meet! How exactly did you get to Perry Ford?"

"Pardon the interruption, sir, but Greystone is under siege!" Sana cut in hastily. "The Sheriff formally requests the Haven's aid."

Kandar was perplexed. "Under siege? By whom?"

Christopher sighed. "All in good time. A scholar like you can surely name one thing that always brings dragons. This time, it also brought thousands of goblin hordes from the Frost Mountains."

Kandar rubbed his smooth chin. "I heard you were looking for clues, not the answer to the mystery itself. Well, Angela will want this contained so we can get three airships to Greystone in four hours-"

"But it'll be too late!" Manny was urgent. "There's another dragon left out there! Who knows how long the defenders will last?"

Kandar frowned. "It'll take an hour to marshal our forces and another three to get to Greystone. And believe me, young man, that's rushing it. Now Christopher, can you tell me the location of the... Cause of these dragons?"

Christopher nodded at Hope, who quickly drew her rumpled cloak closer to shield the Dagger from prying eyes.

Kandar sighed. "You poor soul. My heart goes out to you and your family."

"Oh, I'm sure they're alright. We left from Braddock before-"

"I'm sorry, time to go!" Kandar proclaimed before she could finish. "We've got a city to liberate."

Hope's expression soured in annoyance at Kandar's rudeness, but her frame lost its rigidity as Manny wrapped an arm around her. They stood silently beside Christopher, staring out the window to behold the shrinking world below.

Chapter 10: Unwelcome Revelations

The goblins had fallen back from Greystone's wall not long after the dragon's descent, a move they seemed to realize was its last. Gazing at the enemy lines from atop the wall, Hikaru guessed that they hoped for the return of the other beast that had helped them lay waste to the countryside. The fall of this dragon would be the end of the failed siege of Greystone, the Battle of Skurlag's Folly, as it were.

Evening approached quickly, and Hikaru grew more wary of the arrival of yet another dragon, who would have the advantage over a crowd of soldiers fainting from hunger and exhaustion. Its fortune chasing Christopher would bite either way, lashing out in frustration that it had not captured the Dagger or empowered for indefatigable conquest by the spirit of the Locust trapped within its new toy.

"Minister!" Taro beckoned Hikaru to meet a messenger.

Hikaru recognized the courier from a route that circled the city. "What news have you from the other side?"

"We've seen airships in the distance!" The panting runner downed a jug of water while scarfing down a slice of bread. "If a dragon doesn't get to them, they'll be here in minutes!"

"Well, then, the battle's over!" Hikaru laughed, unstrapping his helmet and hanging it by his side. "We must prepare the city to receive our liberators. Taro, warn the Judge!"

Hikaru turned to see the airships in the distance, vague dots constantly increasing in size as they approached Greystone. The goblins began yapping in the fields beyond the city, a sign of distress that replaced their usual howls. Turning his gaze back on the highway, the return of the wedding dress caused Hikaru to grit his teeth, though the sight of a human amidst the standard-bearers tempted him to hope for the Sheriff's wellbeing.

Taro was cautiously optimistic. "Should I assemble a party to meet them?"

Hikaru pursed his lips. "Let them come to us." He ordered the archers to stand down during the negotiations and directed Wallace to lead him through a nearby postern so that he could meet the goblins outside of the main gate. The standard-bearers nervously approached, keeping their human captive on a tight leash with a bag over his head to preclude easy escape. Hikaru rested his hand on a replacement sword from the Hirose Hotel's army, ready to cut the Sheriff free and run back behind the wall under cover of crossbow fire.

The armored goblin who had met Hikaru during the Sheriff's capture bowed his head, revealing a curious understanding of official greetings in Nara. "It takes boldness to stand alone before your foes. You are not the warlord I expected to battle. If not for you, Greystone would be rubble, Enchanter.

Hikaru smirked. "You and your kind are learning to fear the civilized world again, bakemono. The raids on the hill country end now."

The goblin snickered, and Hikaru mused that its eyes would have rolled if they were not pure obsidian. "It is only the men in the sky who frighten me. But it is no matter to the Locust. The time has come, and we shall all be one again. I just wanted to give you a parting gift, a token of my admiration for your strategy, Enchanter."

Hikaru gripped his sword hilt uneasily. "Just like that? You're letting him go?"

The goblin removed the bag from Juan's head to reveal a multitude of cuts and bruises. "Let no one say that Skurlag of Grennan thinks himself an unbeatable foe. We've had our way with you, now let us return to face our enemies from the Haven." Juan groaned as he was shoved forward, and Hikaru placed his arm around the Sheriff while drawing his sword. Without another word, the goblins dropped their standard and loped away, ready to face certain doom.

"Don't worry, Juan, you're safe now!" Hikaru received no response from the trembling Sheriff, hurrying toward the postern with him.

"How are my men?" Juan could barely speak.

Hikaru sighed. "Save your strength. Know they fought well. One of your constables, Wallace, fought particularly well."

Juan groaned as they walked through the postern. "Wallace? You mean Winston?"

Hikaru raised an eyebrow as Juan's soldiers cheered the return of their leader, lining up to pat him on the back while he graciously returned their affection with smiles and pleased groans.

"Sheriff, I have something for you." Wallace waded through the crowd to greet his fearless leader. "It's a gift." He unsheathed the unusually ornate sword from his belt. Caught up admiring the craftsmanship, Hikaru barely had time to recognize Wallace whispering. "From Skurlag." Hikaru was frozen with horror as Wallace speedily plunged the sword into Juan's chest.

Wallace was immediately seized and beaten beyond recognition by his comrades while Hikaru and others tended to the injured Sheriff. Taro finally beat his way into the scrum and restrained Wallace, calling for chains while the suddenly manic soldier began to froth at the mouth. A physician was quickly summoned, who brought the Sheriff to the a nearby makeshift infirmary. Little time passed before the Sheriff started coughing up blood, and Hikaru knew that he would soon breathe his last breath.

Marching out the hospital door in despair, Hikaru found little joy at the sight of airships casting shadows while descending onto the battlefield. Mounting the wall, he watched two ships settle over the amassed goblins, dropping cargoes of airborne troops to clear safe landing spots that would become forward operating bases. One ship landed at the bottom of the road leading into the hill country, a curious choice given the distance from the rest of the front.

Hikaru prayed that he would find the Sheriff's son on one of the ships, thankfully feeling led to meet the airship in the foothills. Summoning a horse, he rode along the deserted northern highway as fast as he could until he had reached the airship. The crew appeared to be feeding a party of refugees, with whom Hikaru saw Christopher and his charges mingling. One older woman looked similar to Lauren, and he guessed they could be refugees from Braddock and other towns in the hill country attacked by dragons after Hope departed.

The Enchanter smiled at the sight of Hikaru, but he shook his head. "Christopher! Where's the boy?"

Manny jumped up and waved his hand. "I'm here! How goes the battle?"

Hikaru reached down his hand. "Mount my horse now! It's your father, make haste!" When the boy stood still in shock, Hikaru jumped from his horse and rushed through the crowd, grabbing him by the shoulder.

Christopher was aghast. "What in the name of the world happened?"

Hikaru helped a dazed Manny onto his steed. "He hasn't got much time!" They galloped back to the city, neither saying anything as the young man seemed to realize his father's fate. Once they arrived in the city, every soldier paused from their duties and kneeled out of respect. The defenders of Greystone had a profound love for their commander that Hikaru found rare, even among the troops of more famed generals.

Hikaru called through the entrance of the hospital when they arrived. "Is he alive?"

Manny suddenly seemed to snap out of his confusion, hurrying through the entrance and sobbing immediately once they were led to Juan's bedside. Joining the boy, Hikaru was relieved that the Sheriff was still breathing, though the air flowed through increasingly shallower breaths.

Manny finally held back the tears for a moment. "You can't leave now, father."

Juan gasped. "There has... Never been... A better time."

Manny blubbered through his words. "Wh-what do you mean?"

Juan struggled to speak. "You... Just... Chose... Path. To be... Enchanter."

Manny dried a tear on his cheek. "And you're not... Disappointed?"

His father weakly shook his head and stroked his son's hair one last time. "Make... Your... Father... Proud."

Manny burst into tears again as his father left the living world, and Hikaru squeezed his shoulder in comfort. Thinking back to the past week's events, from the attack at Dead Falls to an unexpected betrayal, Hikaru saw that the old world order present at the start of his tour through Manifest was about to collapse. Greystone was merely the first casualty in a war for the Hemisphere now that the Dagger was in such vulnerable hands. Soon, the world would mourn a million fathers just as Manny did, surviving a million monsters only to fall at the hands of a million traitors caught in the grip of the Locust, just like Wallace. The seeds of distrust from every unwelcome dream that one's neighbor was secretly their enemy would grow into unimaginable chaos just as the Locust marshaled his forces. Hikaru just hoped there were enough sound minds to keep the peace because the world had too few Havens to arrive and save the day.

Hope was disheartened to see that the immaculate gardens of the Hirose Hotel had not survived the siege of Greystone, and she wondered what exactly had ruptured the ground beneath it. Trees were uprooted, statutes had fallen over, and fish rotted on the ground sometime after the last drop of water had brought life to their gills. She had seen a few similar ruptures walking through the streets, but nothing like this — and she hoped that her friends had survived whatever disaster befell them.

"Christopher, if anything happened to my girl, you will not see twilight." Flora's promise caused the Enchanter to gulp in fear.

Nothing yet had broken the disquieting silence that covered both her and Terry since the refugees from Braddock had arrived, and Hope sensed agreement with Christopher's judgment that Flora was distressed enough to kill. When they met, Hope saw a look of complete anguish on Terry's face. At the same time, Flora was stoically dismissive, neither answering questions about Caleb's whereabouts. Hope did not want to assume the worst, not after she had gone through so much to save her friends; her grandfather was likely just injured, resting somewhere as he waited for help to arrive. Obviously, Flora and Terry would not want to make Hope jealous of the reunions that would follow with their own wards.

"Oh Hope, you made it!" They were surprised to see Varsha run from the hotel entrance, unexpectedly seated beside Laura and Yukio. She wrapped her arms tightly around Flora and smiled in relief at Hope.

"Wait, Mom, is that you?" Lauren's jaw dropped as she approached, barely recognizing her aunt dressed in tattered, dust-caked clothes. In a rare moment of vulnerability, she swung her arms around Terry and Hope, holding back tears as she revealed sorrow over their separation.

"Don't worry, I'm here now." Terry patted her niece on the back while extending her other arm around Hope. "I'm – we're here for all of you."

This sentiment chilled Hope, and she grew uncomfortable at the idea that Caleb's fate was worse than she imagined. Perhaps he lay alone at Dead Falls, mortally wounded and carrying on just long enough to part with his granddaughter before his last breath… No! Hope could not bear to despair anymore, not when the foul talisman strapped to her belt was turning her into something dark. She had to be positive while positivity remained in her soul, and she looked forward to her grandfather's reassurance of a pleasant future.

Only a matter of time before grandfather arrives, Hope thought. She pulled back from Varsha's embrace to find a seat, espying Christopher lazing about on a bench he had lifted from the ground. He smiled weakly as Hope sat beside him, but the Enchanter stared off into the distance, disagreeably pensive.

If he's gone, we'll make them pay. The thought shook Hope, and she pulled her hand from the Dagger with a yelp, having absent-mindedly begun stroking its hilt once again. How she wished to remove it from herself forever, throwing it into the fires of a distant volcano if needed. Until such a time as the link was broken, Hope knew that she was cursed to be tempted by the spirit within the Locust's talisman, manifesting its power in moments of weakness.

Hope finally took a deep breath and waited, taking the plunge over the cliff, knowing she would find nothing good. "Where is my grandfather?"

"We'll all need to sit down for this." Flora moved away from Varsha and picked up another fallen bench. "Girls, there wasn't some sort of earthquake, was there?"

"Well, we had a little fun with some wyrms." Varsha laughed and set up another bench for Lauren and Terry. "

"You left them here with wyrms outside!" Flora could barely restrain herself from lunging at Christopher in anger.

"I told you, I-"

"Oh, never mind!" Flora was content for the time just to have her daughter at her side. "And pardon me, can I help you, madame?" Flora stared curiously at the silent Yukio, unsure of where she fit.

Varsha introduced them to Yukio, who bowed before leaving them to their privacy. "Yukio was a great friend to us on the journey. We'll have to write to her when we return home."

Hope felt uncomfortable, and she demanded news of her grandfather's health. "What happened to him? Please, I can't bear it any longer!"

Terry grimaced. "Hope, what we have to tell you is... difficult, to say the least. Just know that we are here to comfort you. Anything you need shall come from us, don't hesitate."

"What's keeping grandfather?" Hope could not stand another second in the dark. "I assume he's not far away..."

"Um... " Flora sighed long and hard. "There's no easy way to say this, Hope, so to hell with it! They came for Braddock the day after you left – goblins, dragons, a couple witches – and Caleb..." She paused, wiping a tear from her eye. "Your mother's sword was in his hand as he slew his last foe. And because..." She began to breathe heavily, unable to continue speaking.

"Because of his sacrifice, the school was saved." Terry trembled as she finished the story. "The village is gone, but the youth survived, all because of him."

This was the moment of truth. Hope sat absolutely still, unable to loosen herself from the marble bench that joined itself to her heart of stone. The air withdrew from her lungs like some great boot had been planted firmly on her chest, crushing her frame forever. *Why wasn't I there?* Hope had the blade that would command the enemy's armies; surely, she could have drawn the dragons elsewhere! What good was the Dagger of the Locust if his minions sought the death of its bearer?

For a moment, she looked at her surroundings, the caring women in front of her and the cowardly Enchanter at her side. He would have been more than a match for the invaders, if only he had kept his promise to her grandfather. A frown was sculpted onto her brow as she slowly turned toward Christopher, prepared to strike precisely the blow that would

—

"Hope!" In a flurry of motion, Hope found herself pinned against the ground, Varsha restraining her arm as the Dagger fell from her hands. It had never left her grasp, not even when she thought she was rid of it. This was the moment for tears – all at once, the floodgates of her eyes burst open, and Hope almost worried that she would drown. Varsha gently helped her up, but Hope had little energy to do more than slump against Varsha on the seat that Flora had vacated.

Was he really gone? No more Caleb Defoe, the one man who could still tell her about her mother? Both the doting moments when he brought her a new novel and his grumpy requests for dinner were permanently removed from her life. Hope was alone, claimed as a child only by the demon that had accosted her and Sana in Trumaria. The daughter of a warrior, the granddaughter of a historian, now the child of no one – Hope would so remain unless she had the luck of attracting a husband.

Lauren spoke first. "So... where does that leave us?" The words were garbled in Hope's ears, but she took in enough to understand.

Christopher hesitantly replied. "Your lives are your own to live, but I have an offer for you. Flora, isn't there something you ought to tell your daughter?"

Varsha smirked. "Well, I know you're an enchantress; was it something else?" Even Hope jumped at the revelation, somewhat able to sympathize with the impact of the revelation on her friend.

Flora's eyes popped. "How did you know that?"

Varsha playfully rolled her eyes. "I've only been watching you around the house my whole life. I figured you were hiding it for a reason.

Christopher was pleased by the development. "All the more reason for you to join me at Angela's Haven. I promised you all my care years ago, and if overseeing your tutelage myself at Angela's Haven is the cost, so be it."

Lauren was surprised by his sacrifice. "You can't just abandon your post at Byeong's Haven! Besides, I've still got to prepare for the National Academy –"

Christopher laughed. "National Academy? You'll learn all they have to teach you in one day at the Haven! Besides, Hope will only find peace at the hands of Angela, so she will certainly be going to the Haven. I have a feeling that you would much prefer to become a Professor, Lauren. And you a Ranger, Varsha."

Terry shook her head. "But Christopher! Just because they become students doesn't mean we'll have a place there! I couldn't stand to be away from my child much longer."

Flora smiled at Terry. "You can share a bunk with me, they'll welcome back an old Enchantress."

Christopher winked. "Of course, a Knight of Janis would be most welcome to reside in the Haven."

"Wait, a Knight?" Lauren pulled away from her mother's side, jaw dropping to the ground.

Terry curtly dismissed Christopher's remark. "I'd be just fine as a scullery maid. Not like there aren't dishes to clean in a Haven."

Christopher smiled warmly. "I still have some pull there, and I'll see that you all receive care. Half the population of a Haven are servants, and Terry shall have ample work and pay. It is a privilege earned only because the three of you young ladies each possess a tie to the Great Powers, something your parents saw from an early age. Lauren, as I said, you're a natural Professor, and Varsha seems practically born to be a Ranger."

"And I'm a witch." Hope sighed, finally arriving at the presence of mind to speak.

Christopher shook his head vigorously. "By the powers, no! The fact that you can wield the Dagger without going feral means there's power inside you to contain evil. Angela will help you grow that power."

Hope remained sad. "Everything I remember seems to be an eternity away. I can't stand this awful talisman, filling my head with unwelcome dreams! There's nothing that can get it out of my soul." She tore at the locks of her hair in frustration before bowing her head again, tilting her head to glance at the unsheathed Dagger still lying on the ground.

Christopher offered a reassuring smile. "Angela will help you learn to bear the pain in time. And you won't be alone."

Hope exchanged smiles with Lauren and Varsha. "Well, I will have my friends."

Christopher nodded. "Lauren and Varsha shall never be far. And I will be training Manny myself. We will all be here for you."

"Manny will be there?" Hope finally felt a glimmer of joy. "Do you know what happened to his father?"

Christopher sighed. "No, but I fear the worst. At least he had his father's blessing to train with us, and I believe he'll be my fittest pupil yet!"

"I must go to him at once!" Hope weakly stood up from her seat. "I... I assume we're staying here tonight?"

Christopher nodded. "Yes, once you and Manny have comforted each other, we shall have a night of rest. Come, I'll take you to him."

Lauren and Varsha tried to smile, weak bandages for a friend torn asunder by the news that her home was gone. Hope had an amiable path forward at the Haven, living a life many would envy. Still, she felt the whole affair meaningless without her grandfather. Her heart ached as she jealously regarded Lauren and Varsha clinging to their guardians, and she bristled at the thought of embracing Christopher in Caleb's place.

Hope bade her friends farewell before following the Enchanter to the infirmary, where Manny was likely also finding himself an orphan. Perhaps they would hold each other for a while, glued together by intertwined sorrow. This path of pain was setting Hope on the road to becoming a hero just as tragic as Jasmine the Wanderer, an unwelcome cost for her greatest wish.

"Wait a second." Hope was startled as they neared the exit of the hotel courtyard. "I almost left it behind." She moved slowly at first, hesitant to reunite with the talisman, but she could not keep from the Dagger for long, almost out of breath when she sighed in relief to return it to its sheath.

"You're welcome."

Epilogue: Unwelcome Omissions

"Are you sure she is ready?" Angela's voice had a way of filling every corner of her throneroom while remaining as soft as her chair's unfilled cushions.

Christopher winced as though recalling an indiscretion. "You don't prepare someone for this kind of destiny. Especially not a young girl. Of the few people physically capable of wielding a talisman, adolescent human women are at the bottom of the scale." He milled about the throneroom nervously, joined by Hikaru and the Lady of the Haven in moving around.

"Indeed. My companion tells me that the odds of her being able to use it properly are only a little higher than her discovering it in the first place." Angela smiled at a moving portrait on the wall of the throneroom, the subject smiling back at its decadently dressed master. "Hikaru, you've gained the most from this turn of events. After Christopher took your desired commission, we believed you would be done with the Havens for good."

Hikaru smiled, avoiding the smugness brimming inside. "My gain is Shaolin's loss. And I must still be appointed to a full term by the Council of Janis."

Angela chuckled. "A formality. You shall not be challenged."

Hikaru continued containing his joy. "It will be a return to my favorite vocation - not that I haven't enjoyed writing reports for Empress Takara."

Angela nodded. "Indeed! I am jealous of your insight, and now the Havens will benefit. You must tell me two things concerning my Haven."

"Those are?"

Angela pensively ran a finger through her auburn hair. "The identity of Skurlag, and the potential for more humans to follow the Locust.

Hikaru looked at Christopher, who nodded to him to give their report. "We both initially suspected it to be a witch, but a dark magician would take more pride in attacking Greystone than the still unidentified Skurlag. Everything the Deathlords gained, the fear of invasion, the horror of infiltration, the coming chaos in Yorkton... All seems to be the handiwork of a phantom. None of our friends at Haven outposts worldwide have even seen anything celebratory at the Deathlord strongholds. Without knowing more about the witch, we don't know who else she was bewitching. And we found no trace of the lead goblin that kidnapped the Sheriff to torture for intelligence."

Angela nodded. "It was likely an underling from Grennan that grew tired of its low status and sought to become master of the hill country. A difficult feat without dark magic, but the goblins there are far enough removed from a Deathlord fortress to simply be feral but not possessed. A well-armed battalion could organize them quickly, especially with the help of a witch, giving them a taste for order as they plundered travelers on the highway."

Christopher sighed. "What troubles me about this one is that he was able to transport Cimarron wyrms this far without anyone noticing. They have never been known to travel beyond the scrublands."

Angela gritted her teeth. "Ah yes, the wyrms. You'll have to tell me more about how exactly they were defeated. I believe your former pupil played a part in their demise, Minister?"

Hikaru nodded. "Just more to investigate. I'm glad my servant Yukio has found a place in your court, she will make a wonderful stenographer. She can tell you all you need to know about how the wyrms were defeated."

Angela darted her eyes suspiciously toward Christopher. "Two young women with access to few books in a forest village somehow knew exactly what it would take to defeat ten monsters from a faraway desert. Now you claim one possesses the intellect to be a Professor, and the other the resourcefulness to be a Ranger. Most of all, this... Hope has managed to wield the Dagger of the Locust without being consumed by any sort of dark magic yet?"

Hikaru tried to diffuse Angela's suspicions. "It is quite strange that three 'natural' channelers of the Great Powers would grow up together in the same small town like that, but stranger stories have been destined."

Christopher deflected quickly. "Perhaps Braddock is a magnet for such oddities. In fact, I believe a woman there - a constable - may be an immortal human."

Angela and her portrait exchanged shocked looks and raised eyebrows with one another but did not comment. "Well, Christopher, we will speak much more about your wards before the Council of Janis next year. I will raise Hope as my own until then so that the Council can finally learn the nature of this talisman. But I will ask you now and only now: is there something you're not telling me?"

Christopher hesitated, likely worried that omissions would harm his wards in the future. "Everything I have told you is the truth. "

Hikaru shrugged in acceptance, but Angela frowned sternly. "Christopher, there will come a time when you wish you had answered the question I just asked."

About the Author

Alex McHaddad
A graduate of College of the Canyons and
Eastern Oregon University, Alex lives in rural Oregon
where he enjoys reading, writing, and exploring the
Pacific Northwest wilderness. Learn more about Alex,
his books, and his author interview podcast *Magic For
Us* online at www.magic4.us.

Published Works

Sands of Jannah: Ignoble

Beaver State Confidential

Fallen Blades: Unwelcome Dreams

www.ingramcontent.com/pod-product-compliance
Lightning Source LLC
Chambersburg PA
CBHW050345030726
47503CB00008B/2616